UNWIN HYMAN SHORT STORIES

IS PIGS

**INCLUDING
FOLLOW ON
ACTIVITIES**

EDITED BY TREVOR MILLUM

Published in 1988 by
Unwin Hyman Limited
15/17 Broadwick Street
London W1V 1FP

Reprinted 1990

British Library Cataloguing in Publication Data

Pigs is Pigs———(Unwin Hyman Short Stories)
  1. Short, stories, English
  I. Millum, Trevor
  823'01'08 (FS)   PR1301

  ISBN 0 7135 2814 1

Typeset by TJB Photosetting Ltd., South Witham, Lincolnshire
Printed in Great Britain by
Billing & Sons Ltd., Worcester
Series cover design by Iain Lanyon
Cover illustration by Neil Bennett © 1987

Series editor: Roy Blatchford

Advisers: Jane Leggett and Gervase Phinn

CONTENTS
Page

Introduction

Fiction has always been a major resource for teachers and students involved in the study of language and literature. Perhaps its most important contribution has been the enjoyment and pleasure that readers gain. Equally, fiction has been used because of its power to engage attention and the imagination, and give shape to personal experiences and expectations.

Many of the issues we wish to discuss with students are complex, challenging and probing. Reading fiction provides a chance to consider and reflect on them from a distance, before moving into the realm of personal experience and opinion. Fiction also offers a wealth of models of writing and expression that can be used to assist students in their own writing.

The aim of this collection is to provide a resource for students studying English and English Literature for the General Certificate of Secondary Education.

The stories in this collection will be accessible to students who are not the most able, and a large number will readily engage and hold the attention of even the 'reluctant reader'.

Nevertheless, the stories are not facile and several are quite challenging. All of them are tightly structured and crisply ended, appealing to all readers, whether reluctant or otherwise. They are all excellent examples of the genre.

'The Harry Hastings Method' is an amusing story which will entertain *any* fourth or fifth year pupil as will the slightly more difficult 'Pigs Is Pigs' (which benefits from being read aloud) and 'Hey You Down There!' This last is an absurd and macabre story of an ill-matched couple related with a good dash of wry humour. Domestic stresses also lead to a startling and somewhat grizzly conclusion in 'Late Home'.

'See Me In Me Benz And T'ing' deals with class hatred in Jamaica from the viewpoint of one of the privileged while 'Out On The Wire' and 'Double Vision' confront the conflicts, amongst others, of the classroom. These two stories are more complex than most in the collection, partly because of the flashback techniques employed and partly because of the relationships they explore. 'Incident In The Ghobashi Household' relates sensitively the situation of an unmarried Egyptian girl who is pregnant—an unusual slant on a familiar problem.

The remaining four stories all demonstrate the quality of making the unlikely or impossible appear believable. All have great appeal to fourteen- to sixteen-year-olds. They include the classic science fiction chase story of 'The Ruum'; a tale told entirely in letters and computer printed replies, 'Computers Don't Argue'; a ghost story and a hanging, 'Crossing Over' and 'The Cure'.

In spite of the subject matter of 'The Cure', no one could complain in either this story or any of the others of offensive language or content. Indeed, one of the aims of compiling this anthology has been to gather together those stories which I have found most appeal to older secondary pupils of all abilities, whilst avoiding those whose language or overt concern with violence or sexual situations many teachers find unsuitable for shared reading.

In the Follow On section I have tried to vary the activities so that there is always something suitable for less able or less motivated pupils as well as more demanding items. Many of the suggestions require or lend themselves to a variety of oral work.

They also offer a range of approaches which will help students of all abilities, whether in building up a coursework folder or in preparing for essays written under examination conditions. More specifically, the activities aim to encourage students to:

— work independently and collaboratively

— consider:
    the short story as a genre
    language and style of a writer
    structure and development of plot
    development of character
    setting

— examine the writer's viewpoint and intentions

— respond critically and imaginatively to the stories, orally and in writing

— read a variety of texts, including quite difficult ones

— read more widely.

One important footnote: the activities are divided under three broad headings—*Before, During* and *After Reading*. The intention is that students should engage with the text as closely as possible, from predicting storylines to analysing character's motivations. Teachers using the collection are therefore recommended to preview the Follow On section before reading the stories with students.

The Harry
Hastings Method

Susie Plimson says I should keep on practising my writing. She's been my teacher at Hollywood High Adult Education in the professional writing course and says I am still having trouble with my syntaxes and my tenses, and very kindly gave me private lessons at her place, and she is dark haired and very pretty and about my age (which is twenty-five).

Susie says if I really want to be a professional writer, I should write about what I really know about—if it is interesting—and while I did do a spell in the navy some time back, I was on a destroyer tender and never heard a shot fired except in practice, which I don't think is a highly interesting matter to describe.

But one thing I know a lot about is working the houses in the Hollywood hills. The people who live up there are not particularly stinking rich, but then, I've never been interested in valuable paintings or diamond necklaces, anyway, because what do you do with them?

But there are usually portable radios and TV sets and tape decks and now and then there is some cash lying around, or a fur, or a few pieces of fairly good jewellery, or maybe a new leather jacket – all things easy to dispose of.

This is an area of winding streets and a lot of trees and bushes, and the houses are mostly set back from the street and are some distance from their neighbours, and so it is an easy vicinity to work.

There's no bus service up there at all, so everybody needs a car or two, and if there is no auto in the carport, you can be pretty sure that no one is home.

There are rural-type mailboxes on the street, and people are always stuffing them with business cards and circulars, like ads for house cleaning and landscaping and such.

So I had a lot of cards printed for various things, like for a house-painting firm, and some for the 'Bulldog Burglar Protection Agency', which say we will install all kinds of silent burglar alarms, and bells will ring in our office and we will have radio cars there in a few minutes.

I also have some Pest Control and House Repair cards. None of these firms exists, of course, but neither do the phone numbers on my cards.

But while I drive slowly around the hills in my little VW bus and put my cards in the boxes, I can get a pretty good idea of who is home and who isn't, and who is gone all day, and so forth.

By the way, my truck is lettered with: H. STRUSSMAN INC, GENERAL HOUSE REPAIRS on one side and FERGUSON PEST CONTROL, EVERYBODY LOVES US BUT YOUR PESTS! on the other side.

I make these up myself. My theory is that nobody can ever see both sides of my truck at the same time, which will really confuse witnesses, if there are any. Of course I change the truck signs every week, and every month I paint the truck a different colour.

When I decide that a certain house is ripe for hitting, I go up and ring the doorbell. If I am wrong and someone is home – this is seldom – I ask them if their house happens to be swarming with disease-infested rats. Since there are no rats at all in these hills, they always say no and I leave.

If nobody answers the doorbell, it is, of course, another matter. Most of these houses have locks that could be opened by blindfolded monkeys. Not one of them has any kind of burglar alarm.

There are watchdogs in some houses, but these I avoid, because you never know a friendly dog from a vicious one until you've been chewed up. And, of course, I would not hurt any dog if you paid me.

What I am getting to is about one particular house up there. It's a fairly new one-storey modern style, up a driveway, but you can see the carport from the street below. In casing the place for some time, I figured that a man probably lived there alone.

There was only one car, a great big new Mercedes, and this man drove off every weekday morning at nine. I saw him a few times and he was a nice-looking gentleman of about forty-five. He was always gone all day, so I guessed he had an office job.

So one day, I drove my truck up the driveway and got out and saw a sign: BEWARE OF THE DOG – and, at the same time, this little pooch comes out of a dog door and up to me, and he is a black bundle of hair and the wiggliest, happiest little puppy you ever saw.

I picked him up and let him lick my face and saw that he had a tag on his collar that read: CUDDLES, MY OWNER IS HARRY HASTINGS. There was also a phone number.

I rang the doorbell, but nobody came. The front-door lock was so stupid that I opened it with a plastic card.

Inside – well, you have never seen such a sloppy-kept house. Not dirty – just sloppy. There was five days' worth of dishes in the sink.

I found out later that this Harry Hastings has a maid who comes and cleans once a week, but meantime, this character just throws his dirty shirts and socks on the floor. What a slob.

I turned out to be right about his living alone. There was only one single bed in use – which, of course, was not made, and I doubt if he makes it from one year to the next. There was no sign of any female presence, which I don't wonder, the way this Hastings lives.

One of his rooms is an office, and this was *really* a mess. Papers all over the desk and also all over the floor. This room stank of old cigarette butts, of which smell I am very conscious

11

since I gave up smoking.

From what I found on his desk, I learned that this Harry Hastings is a TV writer. He writes kind of spooky stuff. I took one of his scripts, to study.

From his income-tax returns, which were lying around for all the world to see, I saw he made nearly $23,000 gross the year before.

But most of the furniture in the house is pretty grubby, and the drapes need replacing, which made me wonder what this character spent all his money on, besides the Mercedes.

He had a new electric typewriter and a great big colour-TV set, which would take four men to move, and a hi-fi, but no art objects or decent silver or gold cufflinks or things like that.

It wasn't till I went through his clothes closet that I found out that most of his money went into his wardrobe. There was about $5000 worth of new apparel in there, most of it hand-tailored and from places like where Sinatra and Dean Martin get their outfits. Very flash and up-to-date.

I tried on a couple of jackets, and it turns out that this Hastings and me are exactly the same size! I mean exactly. These clothes looked like they had been tailored for me alone, after six fittings. Only his shoes didn't fit me, sad to say.

I was very pleased, indeed, I can tell you, as I have always had trouble getting fitted off the rack. Also, I like to dress in the latest fashion when I take Susie to nice pláces.

So I took the entire wardrobe, including shirts and ties. I decided to take the typewriter, which I needed for my writing-class homework. The machine I had kept skipping.

But I wanted to try out the typewriter before I took it, and also, I thought I would leave a note for this Hastings, so he wouldn't think I was some kind of crude thug. So I typed:

> Dear Mr Hastings,
> I am typing this to see if your typewriter works OK.
> I see that it does. I am not taking it to sell but I need
> it because I am trying to become a professional
> writer like you, which I know because I saw your
> scripts on your desk, and I am taking one to help me
> with my work, for studying.

I wish to make you a compliment anent your fine wardrobe of clothes. As it happened, they are like they have been made for me only. I am not taking them to sell them but because I need some good clothes to wear. Your shoes do not fit me, so I am leaving them.

I am also not taking your hi-fi, because there is a terrible screech in the treble. I like your dog, and I will give him a biskit.

A Friend

Well, some three months or so now passed, because there was no sense in hitting Hastings' house again until he had time to get a new bunch of clothes together.

But when I thought the time was ripe, I drove by there again and saw a little VW in the carport, and also, there was a big blonde woman shaking rugs.

I drove up and asked her if her house was swarming with disease-infested rats and she said she didn't think so but that she was only the once-a-week cleaning lady. She sounded Scandinavian. I took note that this was a Wednesday.

I went back the next Monday. No car in the carport. But on the way to the house, there was a new sign, hand-lettered on a board, and it read: BEWARE! VICIOUS WATCHDOG ON DUTY! THIS DOG HAS BEEN TRAINED TO ATTACK AND MEAN IT! YOU HAVE BEEN WARNED! PROCEED NO FARTHER!

Well, this gives me pause, as you can well imagine. But then I remember that this Hastings is a writer with an ingenious and inventive mind, and I do not believe this sign for one moment. Cuddles is my friend.

So I start for the house, and suddenly, this enormous alsatian jumps through the dog door and runs straight at me, growling and snarling, and then he leaps and knocks me down, and sure enough, starts chewing me to pieces.

But then out comes Cuddles, and I am sure there is a dog language, for he woofed at this monster dog as if in reproach, as if to say: 'Knock it off. This is a friend. Leave him alone.' So pretty soon, both dogs are licking me.

13

But when I get to the front door, I find that this Hastings has installed a new, burglar-proof lock. I walk around the house and find that there are new locks on both the kitchen door and the laundry-room door. They must have set Hastings back about seventy-five bucks.

There are also a lot of sliding-glass doors around the house, but I don't like to break plate glass, because I know how expensive it is to replace.

But I finally locate a little louvred window by the laundry-room door, and I find that by breaking only one louvre and cutting the screen, I can reach through and around and open the door.

Inside, I find that the house is just as messy as before. This guy will *die* a slob.

But when I get to his bedroom, here is this note, taped to his closet door. It is dusty and looks like it has been there for months. It says:

> Dear Burglar,
>
> Just in *case* you are the same young man who was in here a few months ago, I think I must tell you that you have a long way to go before you will be a professional writer.
>
> 'Anent' is archaic and should be avoided. A 'wardrobe of clothes' is redundant. It is 'biscuit', not 'biskit'. Use your dictionary!
>
> I know you are a young man, because both my cleaning woman and a nineteen-year-old neighbour have seen you and your truck. If you have gotten this far into my house, you cannot be stupid. Have you ever thought of devoting your talents to something a little higher than burgling people such as me?
>
> Harry Hastings

Inside his closet are two fabulous new suits, plus a really great red-and-blue plaid cashmere sports coat. I take these and am about to leave when I remember there is something I want to tell Hastings.

In his office, there is a new electric typewriter, on which I type:

> Dear Mr Hastings,
>   Thank you for your help. In return, I want to tell you that I read the script of yours I took and I think it is pretty good, except that I don't believe that the man should go back to his wife. I mean, after she tried to poison him three times. This is just my opinion, of course.
>   I do not have a dictionary, so I am taking yours. Thank you.
>
>   A Friend

I, of course, do not take this new typewriter, partly because I already have one and also because I figure he will need it to make money with so he can replace his wardrobe again.

Four months go by before I figure it is time to hit the house again. By this time, my clothes are getting kind of tired, and also the styles have changed some.

This time, when I drive up to the house one afternoon, there is a new hand-lettered sign: THIS HOUSE IS PROTECTED BY THE BULLDOG BURGLAR PROTECTION AGENCY! THERE ARE SILENT ALARMS EVERYWHERE! IF THEY ARE TRIPPED, RADIO CARS WILL CONVERGE AT ONCE! PROCEED NO FARTHER! YOU HAVE BEEN WARNED!

Come on now! I and I alone am the *nonexistent* Bulldog Burglar Protection Agency! I'd put my card in his mailbox! This is really one cheap stinker, this Harry Hastings.

When I get near the house, the dogs come out, and I give them a little loving, and then I see a note on the front door.

> Dear Jack,
>   Welcome! Hope you had a nice trip. The key is hidden where it always has been. I didn't have to go to work today. I've run down the hill to get some scotch and some steaks. Be back in a few minutes. The gals are coming at six.
>
>   Harry

Well, this gives me pause. I finally decide that this is not the right day to hit the house. This could, of course, be another of Hastings' tricks, but I can't be sure. So I leave.

But a few days later, I come back and this same note to Jack is still on the door, only now it is all yellowed. You would think that this lame-brain would at least write a new note every day, welcoming Bert or Sam or Harriet or Hazel or whoever.

The truth is that this Hastings is so damn smart, when you think about it, that he is actually stupid.

The broken louvre and the screen have by now been replaced, but when I break the glass and cut the screen and reach around to open the laundry door, I find that he has installed chains and bolts on the inside.

Well, as any idiot knows, you can't bolt all your doors from the inside when you go out, so one door has to be openable, and I figure it has to be the front door; but the only way I can get in is to break a big frosted-plate-glass window to the left of it and reach through and open the door.

As I said, I'm not happy to break plate glass, but this Hastings has left me no choice, so I knock out a hole just big enough for me to reach through and open the door and go in.

This time, there is *another* note on his closet door:

> Dear Burglar,
>
> Are you incapable of pity? By now, you must be the best-dressed burglar in Hollywood. But how many clothes can you *wear*? You might like to know that my burglary insurance has been cancelled. My new watchdog cost me one hundred dollars and I have spent a small fortune on new locks and bolts and chains.
>
> Now I fear you are going to start smashing my plate-glass windows, which can cost as much as ninety dollars to replace. There is only one new suit in this closet. All my other clothes I keep now either in my car or at my office. Take the suit, if you must, but never return, or you will be sorry, indeed, if you do. I have a terrible revenge in mind.
>
> Harry Hastings

16

P.S. You still have time to reform yourself.

P.P.S. I don't like his going back to his poisoning wife, either. But the network insisted on a 'Happy Ending'.

H.H.

Well, I am not about to fall for all this noise about pity. Any man who has a dog trained to go for me and who uses my own Bulldog Agency against me is not, in my mind, deserving of too much sympathy.

So I take the suit, which is a just beautiful Edwardian eight-button, in grey shark-skin.

Now, quite a few months pass and I begin to feel a little sorry for this character, and I decide to let him alone, forever.

But then, one day, when I am out working, some louse breaks into my own pad, which is three rooms over a private garage in Hollywood. He takes every stitch of clothing I own.

By this time, I am heavily dating Susie Plimson, and she likes good dressers. So, while I am not too happy about it, I decide I have to pay Hastings another visit.

No dogs come out this time when I walk to the front door. But on it is a typed note, which says:

> HELGA! DO NOT OPEN THIS DOOR! Since you were here last week, I bought a PUMA for burglar protection. This is a huge cat, a cougar or a mountain lion, about four feet long, not including the tail. The man I bought it from told me it was fairly tame, but it is *NOT*!
>
> It has tried to attack both dogs, who are OK and are locked in the guest room. I myself have just gone down to my doctor's to have stitches taken in my face and neck and arms. The ferocious puma is wandering loose inside the house.
>
> The SPCA people are coming soon to capture it and take it away. I tried to call you and tell you not to come today, but you had already left. Whatever you do, if the SPCA has not come before you, DO NOT UNDER ANY CIRCUMSTANCES OPEN THIS DOOR!!

Well, naturally, this gave me considerable pause. Helga was obviously the blonde cleaning woman. But this was a Tuesday, and she came on Wednesdays. Or she used to. But she could have changed her days.

I stroll around the outside of the house. But all of the curtains and drapes are drawn, and I can't see in. As I pass the guest-room windows, the two dogs bark inside. So this much of the note on the door is true.

So I wander back to the front door, and I think and I ponder. Is there really a puma in there, or is this just another of Hastings' big fat dirty lies?

After all, it is one hell of a lot of trouble to buy and keep a puma just to protect a few clothes. And it is also expensive, and this Hastings I know by now is a cheapskate.

It costs him not one thin dime to put this stupid note to Helga on his front door and, God knows, it would terrify most anybody who wanted to walk in.

Susie told us in class that in every story, there is like a moment of decision. I figured this was mine.

After about five minutes of solid thought, I finally make my decision. There *is* no puma in there. It's just that Hastings wants me to think that there is a puma in there.

So I decide to enter the house, by breaking another hole in the now replaced frosted-plate-glass window to the left of the front door. So I break out a small portion of this glass.

And I peer through this little hole I've made, and I see nothing. No puma. I listen. I don't hear any snarling cat or anything. No puma. Just the same, there *could* be a puma in there and it could be crouching silently just inside the door, waiting to pounce and bite my hand off when I put it in.

Very carefully, I put some fingers in and wiggle them. No puma. And so I put my arm in and reach and turn the doorknob from the inside and open the door a crack.

No snarl from a puma – whatever pumas snarl like. I open the door a little wider and I call, 'Here, pussy-pussy! Here, puma-puma! *Nice* puma!' No response.

I creep in very cautiously, looking around, ready to jump back and out and slam the door on this beast, if necessary. But there is no puma.

And then I realise that my decision was, of course, right, and there is no lousy puma in this damn house. But still, I am sweating like a pig and breathing heavily, and I suddenly figure out what Susie means when she talks about 'the power of the written word'.

With just a piece of writing, this Hastings transferred an idea from his crazy imagination into my mind, and I was willing to believe it.

So I walk down the hall to his bedroom door, which is shut, and there is *another* typed note on it:

> Dear Burglar,
>   OK, so there is no puma. Did you really think I'd let a huge cat mess up my nice neat house?
>   However, I am going to give you a *serious warning*. DO NOT OPEN THIS DOOR! One of the engineers at our studio has invented a highly sophisticated security device and I've borrowed one of his models.
>   It's hidden in the bedroom and it works by means of ultrasonic waves. They are soundless and they have a fantastically destructive and permanent effect on brain tissues. It takes less than a minute of exposure.
>   You will not notice any brain-numbing effects at once, but in a few days, your memory will start to go, and then your reasoning powers, and so, for your *own* sake DO NOT ENTER THIS ROOM!
>   Harry Hastings

Well, I really had to hand it to this loony character. No wonder he made a lot of money as a writer. I, of course, do not believe *one word* of this, *at all*; therefore, I go into the bedroom and hurry to see if there is any hidden electronic device but, of course, there is not. Naturally.

Then I see another note, on the closet door, and it says:

> Dear Burglar,
>   I don't suppose I should have expected you to believe that one, with your limited imagination and

your one-track mind. By the way, where do you go in all my clothes? You must be quite a swinger.

There are only a few new things in the closet. But before you take them, I suggest you sniff them. You will notice a kind of cologne smell, but this is only to disguise another *odour*. I have a pal who was in chemical warfare, and he has given me a liquid that can be sprayed inside clothing. No amount of dry cleaning can ever entirely remove it.

When the clothes are worn, the heat of the body converts this substance into a heavy gas that attacks the skin and produces the most frightful and agonisingly painful blisters, from the ankles to the neck. Never forget that you have been *warned*.

Harry Hastings

Well, I don't believe this for one moment, and so I open the closet door. All there is is one pair of slacks and a sports coat. But this coat looks like the very same *plaid cashmere* I took before and the rat stole from *me*!

But then I realise this could not be so, but it was just that Hastings liked this coat so much he went out and bought another just like it.

Anyway, I find myself sniffing these. They smell of cologne, all right, but nothing else, and I know, of course, that this kind of gas stuff does not exist at all except in Hastings' wild imagination, which I am coming to admire by now.

As I drive back to my pad, I start to laugh when I think of all the stupid and fantastic things that Hastings has tried to put into my mind today by the power of suggestion, and I realise that he almost succeeded. *Almost*, but not quite.

When I get home and climb the outside stairs to my front door, there are *three envelopes* taped to it, one above another. There are no names on them, but they are numbered, 1, 2, 3. I do not know what in hell all this could be about, but I open 1 and read:

Dear Burglar,
The plaid cashmere coat you have over your arm

right now is *not* a replacement for the one you stole.
It is the *same identical coat*. Think about this before
you open envelope 2.

Harry Hastings

Well, of *course*, I think about this as I stand there with my
mouth sort of hanging open. All of a sudden, it *hits* me! *Harry
Hastings* was the rat who stole all his clothes back! But how did
he know where I *live*? How could he know I was going to hit
his house *today*? My hands are all fumbles as I open 2. Inside
it says:

> Dear Burglar,
> To answer your questions: On your *third* visit to
> my house, my young neighbour saw you and fol-
> lowed you home in his car, and so found out just
> where you live. Later, in my own good time, I easily
> entered this place with a bent paper clip and retrieved
> my own clothes. Today, my neighbour called me at
> my office and said you were inside my house again.
> Later, I phoned him and he said you had come
> out, with my coat. So I've had time to come here and
> write and leave these notes. I also have had time to
> do something else, which you will read about in 3.
>
> Harry Hastings

I open this third envelope very fast indeed, because I figure
that if Hastings knows all this, the fuzz will be along any
minute. In it I read:

> Dear Burglar,
> I got the puma idea from a friend out in the valley
> who has one in a large cage in his yard. Long ago, I
> asked him if I might borrow this huge cat for a day
> sometime, and he said yes and that he didn't like
> burglars, either. He has a large carrying cage for the
> puma. I called him this morning the moment I heard
> you were inside my house, and he drove the puma
> right *over here*, and we released the huge cat inside

your place. She is now in there, wandering around loose.

I have done this partly because I am vengeful and vindictive by nature and partly because I've made my living for years as a verisimilitudinous (look it up later) writer, and I deeply resent anyone I cannot fool. The puma that is now inside is my childish way of getting even.

This is no *trick* this time! If you have any brains at *all*, DO NOT OPEN THIS DOOR! Just get out of town before the police arrive, which will be in about half an hour. Goodbye.

Harry Hastings

P.S. The puma's name is Carrie – as if that would help you any.

Well, I read in a story once where somebody was called a 'quivering mass of indecisive jelly', and that is what I was right then. I simply did not know *what* to think or believe. If this was any door but mine, I could walk away. But all my *cash* was hidden inside, and I *had* to get it before I could leave town.

So I stand there and I sweat and I think and I think and after a long time, it comes to me that *this* time, Hastings is finally telling the *truth*. Besides I can hear little noises from inside. There *is* a puma in there! I know it! But I have to get in there, just the same!

I finally figure that if I open the door fast and step back, Carrie might just scoot past me and away. But maybe she will attack me.

But then I figure if I wrap the sports coat around one arm and the slacks around the other, maybe I can fend off Carrie long enough to grab a chair and then force her into my bathroom, the way lion tamers do, and then slam the door on her, and then grab my cash and run out of there, and the police can worry about her when they come.

So this is what I decide to do, only it is some time before I can get up the nerve to unlock the door and push it open. I unlock the door and I stand there. But finally, I think, 'Oh, hell, you *got* to do it, sooner or later,' and so I push my door

22

open and stand back.

No puma jumps at me. Nothing happens at all. But then I look around the corner of my door and *Harry Hastings* is sitting inside. Not with a gun or anything. He is sitting very calmly behind the old card table I use as a desk, with a cigarette in his mouth and a pencil in his hand, and I see one of my stories in front of him.

I walk in and just stand there with my face on and cannot think of any clever remark to make, when he says: 'Tell me one thing. *Did* you or did you *not* really believe there was a puma in here?'

If I remember right – I was pretty shook up then – I nodded and I said, 'Yes, sir. Yes. I really did.'

Then he smiled a big smile and said, 'Well, thank heavens for *that*, I was beginning to think I was losing my grip. I feel a little better now. Sit down. I want to talk to you. By the way, your syntax is terrible and your grammar is worse. I've been making some corrections while waiting for you. However, that's not what I want to talk to you about. Sit down. Stop trembling, will you, and sit down!'

I sat.

As I write now, I am the co-owner and manager of the Puma Burglar Protection Agency. Harry Hastings is my silent partner and he put up two thousand dollars for financing. Susie helps me with my accounts. I have 130 clients now, at five dollars a month each.

The reason it's so cheap is that we use the Harry Hastings Method. That is, we don't bother with burglar alarms or things like that, I just patrol around and keep putting up and changing signs and notices and notes on front doors. Already, the burglary rate in my area has been cut by two-thirds.

This very morning, I got a little letter from Harry Hastings with two new ideas for front-door notes. One is: CLARA! I HAVE ALREADY CALLED THE POLICE AND THEY WILL BE HERE IN MINUTES! DO NOT CALL THEM AGAIN! GEORGE IS LOCKED IN THE BATHROOM AND CAN'T GET OUT, SO WE WILL BE SAFE TILL THEY GET HERE! The second one is: NOTICE! BECAUSE OF A FRIGHT-

FULLY CONTAGIOUS DISEASE, THIS HOUSE HAS
BEEN EVACUATED AND QUARANTINED. IT MUST
ABSOLUTELY NOT BE ENTERED UNTIL IT HAS BEEN
FUMIGATED!

Harry Hastings says that I should be sure to warn the house-
holder to remove this notice before any large parties.

Trevor Millum

*L*ate Home

Where was she *this* time? It was always the same when he wanted to go out. Promises. Yes, I'll be back by then. And then he'd be waiting and looking at the clock and ringing the time and reading the small ads in the Evening Telegraph even though there was nothing he wanted – except to hear the car returning. As ever, his feelings were a mixture of annoyance and anxiety. What if..? And the anxiety heightened the annoyance because he was irritable at being made to worry, like the mother who scolds her child with the words 'Just think of all the worry you've caused us.'

He looked down the road again. The conifer trees at the edge of the path were just visible. It had been dark for some time. Lights and engine noise awakened his spirits. It was the wrong noise: the car went straight past. How much traffic there was whenever you were waiting for someone! He noticed the coleus needed water. It always needed water but he couldn't bring himself to attend to it now. Waiting paralysed his ability to do anything else.

Another car passed. It was now very late. What a reputation he would be getting – remarks, half mocking, half serious, testing his patience even further. When she came he had every right to be angry, very angry. He need have no scruples about giving in to his annoyance this time.

*   *   *

She drove as swiftly as she dared. She was going to be a bit late and he would fuss and complain and probably go off in a bad mood and then all his friends, or colleagues as he called them, would think he was a fool to put up with her – and that she was unreliable and, of course, just like a woman! So what? But she drove a little faster, turning off the heater and opening the window. The stream of brisk evening air disturbed her twenty-five pound hairstyle but again she thought, so what? The black strands wisped in front of her eyes.

The road narrowed and curved. On either side were high, unkempt hawthorn hedges and behind them the remains of old chalk quarries: large white sores that wouldn't heal. Headlights swept towards her. She kept her hands steady and her eyes rigidly on the air just to the left of the lights. At such times she always felt that she had become invisible to the other driver, who would only realise her existence after the impact. The lorry swept past: a gust of hot air and diesel fumes and total unconcern.

The car headlamps picked out figures in the road ahead. There seemed to be two or three people, making no attempt to keep in to the side of the road. She slowed, trying to make out what they were doing. If they didn't move, she was going to hit one of them, the fools... She was about to press the horn button when she saw that one of the figures, a man, dressed in a white T-shirt and dark trousers, was signalling her to stop. She hesitated between panic and calm, between pressing the accelerator and pressing the brake. She stopped, uncertainly but with irritation. She didn't have time to give lifts to people.

They all looked much the same: light-coloured T-shirts with faded emblems and slogans, dark jeans, pale unshaven faces. The first one put his right hand on the window sill of the car and his other hand on the roof. A position of ease and familiarity. He leant down, his head almost through the open window.

'Sorry to stop you. I wonder if you can help us?'

She noticed two drops of sweat on his upper lip. She wanted him to wipe them away, irritated with his presumption and with the delay.

'Yes?' she said, coolly, reservedly, in a manner which suited her high-necked white blouse with the delicate stitching.

'There's someone here who needs to get to the hospital.'

She glanced around. She could only see one person behind him, just the right half of a person in fact – a right half that looked perfectly healthy. Thoughts ran rapidly: there was no one ill or injured – yes there was – she would have to – but he had a dreadful disease, infectious, horrid – he was bleeding – he would die in the car...

'I'm already late—' she started to say, not forcefully enough. Why weren't there any other cars? Where was the traffic, where were the glaring headlights?

'He needs to get to the hospital.' The manner of the statement brought back her annoyance. It was assertive, it assumed a right to travel in her car, her clean car. She was about to say, in her most effective, haughty tone, 'Very well then, I'll telephone for an ambulance at the next call-box,' when she noticed two things almost simultaneously. The third man was at the other side of the car, one hand on the side of the car, one hand on the door handle. The second man had come closer. Her pulse jumped. He was carrying a long bladed knife, like a pruning tool. She thought, but did not say, Help. Her left hand put the car into gear, her right hand tightened on the steering wheel. The man who had been speaking to her started to open her door – indeed, he had both hands round the top of the door frame. A vision of the men climbing into the car on each side of her, crushing her between them, seized her. Without thought and seemingly without effort, she pulled on the door with her right hand, gripped the wheel with her left, pushed down with her right foot and took her left off the clutch. The car leapt forward, roaring.

Then confusion took over. Was she screaming or wasn't she? Had she got away or were they with her somehow? Why was it so awfully noisy? Oncoming lights focussed a part of her mind. She thought of steering, thought of slowing down, realised the car was doing nearly twenty miles an hour in first gear, forced herself to stare ahead, not in the mirror, forced herself to change gear. I'm safe: I've got away. Fear changed into a strange exultation, a sort of childish excitement. She moved into top gear and raced on down the road, turned onto the dual carriageway with a Hollywood screech and kept her foot obstinately on the accelerator pedal.

She had travelled several miles before she recollected that she was not on the right road home. By the time she had found a roundabout other reactions had begun. I'm trembling, she thought. They say that's what happens. It's shock. You tremble. I must stop. I might have an accident.

*   *   *

He sighed. It was a sigh of worry rather than annoyance now. Then he thought things through logically. If she had left at such a time, taken so long to drive, then it would be… and she wasn't all that late, not late enough to signal an accident or a breakdown, just late enough for someone who didn't take enough care about punctuality, who could never say goodbye to anyone, who valued her time more than his. If only her money hadn't paid for half the car, more than half the car! Had he smoked, he would have been lighting cigarette after cigarette now. Instead, he adjusted his tie, combed his hair, ran his fingers through his hair, combed it again, sighed, kicked the plant pot, scraped the polish on his shoe and swore. He brushed at the mark on the leather halfheartedly. The telephone rang.

As he was walking towards the phone, trying not to run, he heard a car – their car. He answered the phone: the second wrong number that evening. The car came up the short drive and stopped alongside the porch. He marched righteously outside. She leant over from the driver's side to greet him, smiling weakly he thought. She slid over to the passenger side, opened the door and was only half out when he spoke.

'Where have you been? Do you know what time it is?'

She said nothing. Her stomach contracted. He would never believe her. How could she say it all? What *had* happened?

'I was stopped—' she began, and took a breath. How could

28

she find the words to say it all?

'Stopped? You're always being made to stop by someone. It's impossible trying to keep arrangements with you. You have no idea...'

She stood by the doorway. He was half in the still open car-door. She wanted to cry but she wouldn't: she suddenly hated him because he didn't care. She wouldn't tell him, then he'd be in the wrong and she'd be in the right.

'I've been worrying— thinking you've had an accident: broken down in some dark street... and you were just taking your time, driving along with the radio on and wondering what excuse to use this time.'

Her resolution to say nothing gave way. 'I was stopped by some men,' she said again. She could smell her own sweat, though the white blouse looked as crisp as ever.

'A good one!' he said, half turning away. 'What did they do, jump out of the telegraph wires on to the roof of the car? Batter their way in through the windscreen?' Pleased with his humour, he slammed the door, slid across to the steering wheel and started to drive away. When he glanced in the mirror she was no longer at the door. Gone in to comb her hair already, he thought, well, tonight I won't worry about being late home.

Inside the house she was in the bathroom, being sick. Reaction, she thought. Shock. But I didn't scream; I just drove away. Yet I remember the sound of screaming.

*   *   *

He arrived at the club, now merely cross in a cold way, a way that wouldn't forgive and forget easily. The car parking attendant came to open the door. As he stepped out, he felt something touch him. Something fell to the ground that had been trapped in the door jamb. Without thinking, he bent and picked it up. It was greyish brown, long and thin. At first he thought it was a vegetable of some sort. Then, with the attendant staring at him, he realised what he held: it was a human finger, wrenched off at the joint.

TREVOR MILLUM

a personal essay

Some people don't like short stories because 'you just get interested and it ends.' For others, the fact that you can digest them at one sitting is the advantage – and if you really enjoy one, you can actually read it again! As a reader, I like the compactness of short stories – and writers are much less likely to be as self-indulgent as they often are in novels; as one pupil said, 'They can't rabbit on.'

I never intended to write short stories, or indeed fiction at all, having put two childhood Biggles-style adventures and one adolescent novel behind me. But I am always writing and when the producer for whom I was broadcasting some book reviews inquired about short stories I started thinking. The special requirements of the short story form – especially with the added restraint that each one fit a fifteen minute radio slot – presented a challenge I couldn't resist. I wrote a few and was hooked.

A writer in an earlier volume in this series, Marjorie Darke, has said, 'One or two characters. A single incident. A brief length of time.' I agree absolutely. Most of my stories have come out of one incident: an imagined or remembered

30

moment. In 'Late Home' that incident is split into two parts: the moment when the woman realises the threat and reacts instinctively and the moment when the finger is discovered. Everything else fits around those scenes. Plot and character grew together. In 'Late Home' the personalities of the two main characters and the relationship between them formed early on and I realised that the feelings of resentment between them were as necessary to make the story work as the basic plot idea of the severed finger.

Other parts of the story may be necessary for quite mundane reasons: like ensuring it all makes sense, is credible within its own terms. For example, the positions the men take up, the fact that the woman partly opens the door and so on. Other parts are not quite so vital; not that they are unimportant, but in the sense that they can be changed. Some of the details of setting, for instance, are there to create a feeling of reality. Nevertheless they can be, and have been, altered. The original tale was set in South East Asia where it was first published. When I rewrote it, the *lorongs* (Malaysian country lanes) and storm drains were removed; chalk quarries and hawthorn hedges were introduced.

Although the characters are, for me as for almost all writers, very important, I prefer to leave them lightly sketched. In many of my stories, including 'Late Home', they have no names. I like the mystery that the anonymity provides and I believe that readers will create their own portraits all the more readily from these sketches if there are no names to prejudice them. Perhaps that is the reason – or maybe I just don't like having to commit myself.

What I do commit myself to is an ending. The ending is often in place long before I decide how to begin. Frequently the rest of the story is a matter of building up curiosity which will only be satisfied in the final sentences (preferably *the* final sentence) of the story. This is a personal preference but one which suits the short story format well.

Although I like my stories to have a definite ending, it is usually clear that this is not the end in any real sense and indeed leaves more questions than it answers. What will the husband do now? What will happen when he gets home? What has happened to the injured man? And so on. For of course an ending is unreal. In life, things go on, but short stories, like novels, are honest falsehoods. You tell the reader that such-and-such a thing happened even though it didn't: it's a lie. But you write it, not only as realistically, as believably, as you can, but as honestly as you can – in the sense that as far as your experience (and intuition and imagination…) goes, this *is* how *that* character would behave in *that* situation. Failure to be honest in this way does, I think, make bad writing.

After all the work – and even a short story is a lot of work – how do you know if it's any good? Your own feelings, having been so closely involved, cannot be fully trusted. Friends and relations are kind and polite…and therefore unreliable. That is why the views of someone else – whom you respect but who doesn't have to please you – are so important. Sometimes you can find this kind of response in a group of fellow writers or a teacher. That is why the positive reaction of a publisher is so significant, rather than for fame or fortune – rarities even for published writers.

The really testing time comes when the story is out of your control, when it is in the hands and then the minds of real readers. That is a wonderful moment, a worrying moment, but also a frustrating one – because only rarely do you discover what that audience is making of it. You have set the story free, like a pupil who has left school, and the only thing to do is to hope to hear from it (or of it) from time to time and get down to starting afresh.

ELLIS PARKER BUTLER
'Pigs Is Pigs'

Mike Flannery, the Westcote agent of the Interurban Express Company, leaned over the counter of the express office and shook his fist. Mr Morehouse, angry and red, stood on the other side of the counter, trembling with rage. The argument had been long and heated, and at last Mr Morehouse had talked himself speechless. The cause of the trouble stood on the counter between the two men. It was a soap-box across the top of which were nailed a number of strips, forming a rough but serviceable cage. In it two spotted guinea-pigs were greedily eating lettuce leaves.

'Do as you loike, then!' shouted Flannery; 'pay for thim an' take thim or don't pay for thim and leave thim be. Rules is rules, Misther Morehouse, an' Mike Flannery's not goin' to be called down fer breakin' of thim.'

'But, you everlastingly stupid idiot!' shouted Mr Morehouse, madly shaking a flimsy printed book beneath the agent's nose, 'can't you read it here—in your own plain printed rates? "Pets, domestic, Franklin to Westcote, if properly boxed, twenty-five cents each."' He threw the book on the counter in disgust. 'What more do you want? Aren't they pets?

Aren't they domestic? Aren't they properly boxed? What?'

He turned and walked back and forth rapidly, frowning ferociously. Suddenly he turned to Flannery and, forcing his voice to an artificial calmness, spoke slowly but with intense sarcasm.

'Pets,' he said. 'P-e-t-s! Twenty-five cents each. There are two of them. One! Two! Two times twenty-five are fifty! Can you understand that? I offer you fifty cents.'

Flannery reached for the book. He ran his hand through the pages and stopped at page sixty-four.

'An' I don't take fifty cints,' he whispered, in mockery. 'Here's the rule for ut. "Whin the agint be in anny doubt regardin' which of two rates applies to a shipmint, he shall charge the larger. The consign-ey may file a claim for the overcharge." In this case, Misther Morehouse, I be in doubt. Pets thim animals may be, an' domestic they be, but pigs, I'm blame sure they do be, an' me rules says plain as the nose on yer face, "Pigs, Franklin to Westcote, thirty cints each." An', Misther Morehouse, by me arithmetical knowledge two times thurty comes to sixty cints.'

Mr Morehouse shook his head savagely.

'Nonsense!' he shouted, 'confounded nonsense, I tell you! Why, you poor, ignorant foreigner, that rule means common pigs, domestic pigs, not guinea-pigs!'

Flannery was stubborn.

'Pigs is pigs,' he declared firmly. 'Guinea-pigs or dago pigs or Irish pigs is all the same to the Interurban Express Company an' to Mike Flannery. Th' nationality of the pig creates no differentiality in the rate, Misther Morehouse! 'Twould be the same was they Dutch pigs or Rooshun pigs. Mike Flannery,' he added, 'is here to tind to the expriss business an' not to hould conversation wid dago pigs in sivinteen languages fer to discover be they Chinese or Tipperary by birth an' nativity.'

Mr Morehouse hesitated. He bit his lip and then flung out his arms wildly.

'Very well!' he shouted. 'You shall hear of this! Your president shall hear of this! It is an outrage! I have offered you fifty cents. You refuse it! Keep the pigs until you are ready to take the fifty cents, but, by George, sir, if one hair of those pigs'

34

heads is harmed I will have the law on you!'

He turned and stalked out, slamming the door. Flannery carefully lifted the soap-box from the counter and placed it in a corner. He was not worried. He felt the peace that comes to a faithful servant who has done his duty and done it well.

Mr Morehouse went home raging. His boy, who had been awaiting the guinea-pigs, knew better than to ask him for them. He was a normal boy, and therefore always had a guilty conscience when his father was angry. So the boy slipped quietly around the house. There is nothing so soothing to a guilty conscience as to be out of the path of the avenger.

Mr Morehouse stormed into the house.

'Where's the ink?' he shouted at his wife as soon as his foot was across the door-sill.

Mrs Morehouse jumped guiltily. She never used ink. She had not seen the ink, nor moved the ink, nor thought of the ink, but her husband's tone convicted her of the guilt of having borne and reared a boy, and she knew that whenever her husband wanted anything in a loud voice the boy had been at it.

'I'll find Sammy,' she said meekly.

When the ink was found Mr Morehouse wrote rapidly, and he read the completed letter and smiled a triumphant smile.

'That will settle that crazy Irishman!' he exclaimed. 'When they get that letter he will hunt another job all right.'

A week later Mr Morehouse received a long official envelope, with the card of the Interurban Express Company in the upper left corner. He tore it open eagerly and drew out a sheet of paper. At the top it bore the number A6754. The letter was short. 'Subject—Rate on guinea-pigs,' it said. 'Dear Sir— We are in receipt of your letter regarding rate on guinea-pigs between Franklin and Westcote, addressed to the president of this company. All claims for overcharge should be addressed to the Claims Department.'

Mr Morehouse wrote to the Claims Department. He wrote six pages of choice sarcasm, vituperation, and argument, and sent them to the Claims Department.

A few weeks later he received a reply from the Claims Department. Attached to it was his last letter.

'Dear Sir,' said the reply. 'Your letter of the 16th inst., addressed to this department, subject rate on guinea-pigs from Franklin to Westcote, rec'd. We have taken up the matter with our agent at Westcote, and his reply is attached herewith. He informs us that you refused to receive the consignment or to pay the charges. You have therefore no claim against this company, and your letter regarding the proper rate on the consignment should be addressed to our Tariff Department.'

Mr Morehouse wrote to the Tariff Department. He stated his case clearly, and gave his arguments in full, quoting a page or two from the encyclopaedia to prove that guinea-pigs were not common pigs.

With the care that characterises corporations when they are systematically conducted, Mr Morehouse's letter was numbered, O.K'd. and started through the regular channels. Duplicate copies of the bill of lading, manifest, Flannery's receipt for the package, and several other pertinent papers were pinned to the letter, and they were passed to the head of the Tariff Department.

The head of the Tariff Department put his feet on his desk and yawned. He looked through the papers carelessly.

'Miss Kane,' he said to his stenographer, 'take this letter. "Agent, Westcote, N.J. Please advise why consignment referred to in attached papers was refused domestic pet rates."'

Miss Kane made a series of curves and angles on her notebook and waited with pencil poised. The head of the department looked at the papers again.

'Huh, guinea-pigs!' he said. 'Probably starved to death by this time! Add this to that letter: "Give condition of consignment at present."'

He tossed the papers on to the stenographer's desk, took his feet from his own desk, and went out to lunch.

When Mike Flannery received the letter he scratched his head.

'Give prisint condition,' he repeated, thoughtfully. 'Now what do thim clerks be wantin' to know, I wonder? "Prisint condition," is ut? Thim pigs, praise St Patrick, do be in good health, so far as I know, but I niver was no veterinary surgeon to dago pigs. Mebbe thim clerks wants me to call in the pig docther an' have their pulses took. Wan thing I do know, how-iver, which is they've glorious appytites for pigs of their soize. Ate? They'd ate the brass padlocks off a barn door! If the paddy pig, by the same token, ate as hearty as these dago pigs do, there'd be a famine in Ireland.'

To assure himself that his report would be up to date, Flannery went to the rear of the office and looked into the cage. The pigs had been transferred to a larger box—a dry goods box.

'Wan–two–t'ree–four–foive–six–sivin–eight!' he counted. 'Sivin spotted an' wan all black. All well an' hearty an' all eatin' loike ragin' hippy-potty-musses.' He went back to his desk and wrote.

'Mr Morgan, Head of Tariff Department,' he wrote. 'Why do I say dago pigs is pigs because they is pigs and will be til you say they ain't which is what the rule book says stop your jolly-ing me you know it as well as I do. As to health they are all well and hoping you are the same. P.S. There are eight now the family increased all good eaters. P.S. I paid out so far two dollars for cabbage which they like shall I put in bill for same what?'

Morgan, head of the Tariff Department, when he received this letter, laughed. He read it again, and became serious.

'By George!' he said. 'Flannery is right. "Pigs is pigs." I'll have to get authority on this thing. Meanwhile, Miss Kane, take this letter: "Agent, Westcote, N.J. Regarding shipment guinea-pigs, File No. A6754. Rule 83, General Instruction to Agents, clearly states that agents shall collect from consignee all costs of provender, etc., etc., required for live stock while in transit or storage. You will proceed to collect same from consignee."'

Flannery received this letter next morning, and when he read it he grinned.

'Proceed to collect,' he said softly. 'How thim clerks do loike to be talkin'! *Me* proceed to collect two dollars and twinty-foive cints off Misther Morehouse! I wonder do thim clerks *know* Misther Morehouse? I'll git it! Oh yes! "Misther Morehouse, two an' a quarter, plaze." "Cert'nly, me dear frind Flannery. Delighted!" *Not*!'

Flannery drove the express wagon to Mr Morehouse's door. Mr Morehouse answered the bell.

'Ah,ha!' he cried as soon as he saw it was Flannery. 'So you've come to your senses at last, have you? I thought you would! Bring the box in.'

'I hev no box,' said Flannery, coldly. 'I hev a bill agin Misther John C. Morehouse for two dollars and twinty-foive cints for kebbages aten by his dago pigs. Wud you wish to pay ut?'

'Pay—Cabbages—!' gasped Mr Morehouse. 'Do you mean to say that two little guinea-pigs—'

'Eight!' said Flannery. 'Papa an' mamma an' the six childer. Eight!'

For answer Mr Morehouse slammed the door in Flannery's face. Flannery looked at the door reproachfully.

'I take ut the con-*sign*-y don't want to pay for thim kebbages,' he said. 'If I know signs of refusal, the con-*sign*-y refuses to pay for wan dang kebbage leaf an' be hanged to me!'

Mr Morgan, the head of the Tariff Department consulted the president of the Interurban Express Company regarding guinea-pigs, as to whether they were pigs or not pigs. The president was inclined to treat the matter lightly.

'What is the rate on pigs and on pets?' he asked.

'Pigs thirty cents, pets twenty-five,' said Morgan.

'Then, of course, guinea-pigs are pigs,' said the president.

'Yes,' agreed Morgan. 'I look at it that way too. A thing that can come under two rates is naturally due to be classed as the higher. But are guinea-pigs pigs? Aren't they rabbits?'

'Come to think of it,' said the president, 'I believe they are more like rabbits. Sort of halfway station between pig and rabbit. I think the question is this—are guinea-pigs of the domestic pig family? I'll ask Professor Gordon. He is an authority on such things. Leave the papers with me.'

The president put the papers on his desk and wrote a letter to Professor Gordon. Unfortunately the professor was in South America collecting zoological specimens, and the letter was forwarded to him by his wife. As the professor was in the highest Andes, where no white man had ever penetrated, the letter was many months in reaching him. The president forgot the guinea-pigs, Morgan forgot them, Mr Morehouse forgot them, but Flannery did not. One-half of his time he gave to the duties of his agency; the other half was devoted to the guinea-pigs. Long before Professor Gordon received the president's letter Morgan received one from Flannery.

'About them dago pigs,' it said, 'what shall I do, they are great in family life, no race suicide for them, there are thirty-two now shall I sell them do you take this express office for a menagerie, answer quick.'

Morgan reached for a telegraph blank and wrote:

'Agent, Westcote. Don't sell pigs.'

He then wrote Flannery a letter calling his attention to the fact that the pigs were not the property of the company, but were merely being held during a settlement of a dispute regarding rates. He advised Flannery to take the best possible care of them.

Flannery, letter in hand, looked at the pigs and sighed. The dry-goods box cage had become too small. He boarded up twenty feet of the rear of the express office to make a large and airy home for them, and went about his business. He worked with feverish intensity when out on his rounds, for the pigs required attention, and took most of his time. Some months later, in desperation, he seized a sheet of paper and wrote '160' across it and mailed it to Morgan. Morgan returned it asking for explanation. Flannery replied:

'There be now one hundred sixty of them dago pigs, for heaven's sake let me sell off some, do you want me to go crazy, what?'

Not long after this the president of the express company received a letter from Professor Gordon. It was a long and scholarly letter, but the point was that the guinea-pig was the *Cavia aparaea* while the common pig was the genus *Sus* of the family *Suidae*. He remarked that they were prolific and multiplied rapidly.

'They are not pigs,' said the president, decidedly, to Morgan. 'The twenty-five cent rate applies.'

Morgan made the proper notation on the papers that had accumulated in File A6754, and turned them over to the Audit Department. The Audit Department took some time to look the matter up, and after the usual delay wrote Flannery that as he had on hand one hundred and sixty guinea-pigs, the property of consignee, he should deliver them and collect charges at the rate of twenty-five cents each.

Flannery spent a day herding his charges through a narrow opening in their cage so that he might count them.

'Audit Dept.,' he wrote, when he had finished the count, 'you are way off there may be was one hundred and sixty dago pigs once, but wake up don't be a back number. I've got even eight hundred now shall I collect for eight hundred or what? How about sixty-four dollars I paid out for cabbages?'

It required a great many letters back and forth before the Audit Department was able to understand why the error had been made of billing one hundred and sixty instead of eight hundred, and still more time for it to get the meaning of the 'cabbages.'

Flannery was crowded into a few feet at the extreme front of the office. The pigs had all the rest of the room, and two boys were employed constantly attending to them. The day after Flannery had counted the guinea-pigs there were eight more added to his drove, and by the time the Audit Department gave him authority to collect for eight hundred Flannery had given up all attempts to attend to the receipt or the delivery of goods. He was hastily building galleries around the express office, tier above tier. He had four thousand and sixty-four guinea-pigs to care for! More were arriving daily.

Immediately following its authorisation the Audit Department sent another letter, but Flannery was too busy to open it. They wrote another and then they telegraphed:

'Error in guinea-pig bill. Collect for two guinea-pigs, fifty cents. Deliver all to consignee.'

Flannery read the telegram and cheered up. He wrote out a bill as rapidly as his pencil could travel over paper and ran all the way to the Morehouse home. At the gate he stopped suddenly. The house stared at him with vacant eyes. The windows were bare of curtains and he could see into the empty rooms. A sign on the porch said, 'To Let'. Mr Morehouse had moved! Flannery ran all the way back to the express office. Sixty-nine guinea-pigs had been born during his absence. He ran out again and made feverish inquiries in the village. Mr

Morehouse had not only moved, but he had left Westcote. Flannery returned to the express office and found that two hundred and six guinea-pigs had entered the world since he left it. He wrote a telegram to the Audit Department.

'Can't collect fifty cents for two dago pigs consignee has left town address unknown what shall I do? Flannery.'

The telegram was handed to one of the clerks in the Audit Department, and as he read it he laughed.

'Flannery must be crazy. He ought to know that the thing to do is to return the consignment here,' said the clerk. He tele-graphed Flannery to send the pigs to the main office of the company at Franklin.

When Flannery received the telegram he set to work. The six boys he had engaged to help him also set to work. They worked with the haste of desperate men, making cages out of soap boxes, cracker boxes, and all kinds of boxes, and as fast as the cages were completed they filled them with guinea-pigs and expressed them to Franklin. Day after day the cages of guinea-pigs flowed in a steady stream from Westcote to Franklin, and still Flannery and his six helpers ripped and nailed and packed, relentlessly and feverishly. At the end of the week they had shipped two hundred and eighty cases of guinea-pigs, and there were in the express office seven hundred and four more pigs than when they began packing them.

'Stop sending pigs. Warehouse full,' came a telegram to Flannery. He stopped packing only long enough to wire back, 'Can't stop,' and kept on sending them. On the next train up from Franklin came one of the company's inspectors. He had instructions to stop the stream of guinea-pigs at all hazards. As his train drew up at Westcote Station he saw a cattle-car standing on the express company's siding. When he reached the express office he saw the express waggon backed up to the door. Six boys were carrying bushel baskets full of guinea-pigs from the office and dumping them into the waggon. Inside the room Flannery, with his coat and vest off, was shovelling guinea-pigs into bushel baskets with a coal-scoop. He was winding up the guinea-pig episode.

He looked up at the inspector with a snort of anger.

'Wan waggonload more an' I'll be quit of thim, an' niver will ye catch Flannery wid no more foreign pigs on his hands. No, sur! They near was the death o' me. Nixt toime I'll know that pigs of whativer nationality is domestic pets—an' go at the lowest rate.'

He began shovelling again rapidly, speaking quickly between breaths.

'Rules may be rules, but you can't fool Mike Flannery twice wid the same thrick—whin ut comes to live stock, dang the rules. So long as Flannery runs this expriss office pigs is pets— an' cows is pets an' horses is pets—an' lions an' tigers an' Rocky Mountain goats is pets—an' the rate on thim is twinty-foive cints.'

He paused long enough to let one of the boys put an empty basket in the place of the one he had just filled. There were only a few guinea-pigs left. As he noted their limited number his natural habit of looking on the bright side returned.

'Well, annyhow,' he said cheerfully, ' 'tis not so bad as ut might be. What if thim dago pigs had been elephants!'

CATHERINE STORR

Crossing Over

If she hadn't been fond of dogs, she would never have volunteered for this particular job. When her class at school were asked if they would give up some of their spare time towards helping old people, most of the tasks on offer had sounded dreary. Visiting housebound old men and women, making them cups of tea and talking to them; she hadn't fancied that, and she wasn't any good at making conversation, let alone being able to shout loud enough for a deaf person to hear. Her voice was naturally quiet. She didn't like the idea of doing anyone else's shopping, she wasn't good enough at checking that she'd got the right change. The check-out girls in the supermarket were too quick, ringing up the different items on the cash register. Nor did she want to push a wheelchair to the park. But walking old Mrs Matthews' dog, that had seemed like something she might even enjoy. She couldn't go every evening, but she would take him for a good long run on the Common on Saturdays, and on fine evenings, when the days were longer, she'd try to call for him after school some weekdays. She had started out full of enthusiasm.

What she hadn't reckoned with was the dog himself. Togo

was huge, half Alsatian, half something else which had given him long woolly hair, permanently matted and dirty. Once, right at the beginning, she had offered to bathe and groom him, but Mrs Matthews had been outraged by the suggestion, was sure the poor creature would catch cold, and at the sight of the comb, Togo backed and growled and showed his teeth. It was as much as she could do to fasten and unfasten his leash, and he did not make that easy. The early evening walks weren't quite so bad, because there wasn't time to take him to the Common, so he stayed on the leash all the time. Even then he was difficult to manage. He seemed to have had no training and he certainly had no manners. He never stopped when she told him to, never came when she called him, so that every Saturday, when she dutifully let him run free among the gorse bushes and little trees on the Common, she was afraid she might have to return to Mrs Matthews without the dog, confessing that he had run away. Mrs Matthews did not admit that Togo was unruly and difficult to manage, any more than she would admit that he smelled. It was only a feeling that she shouldn't go back on her promise to perform this small service to the community that kept the girl still at the disagreeable task.

This particular evening was horrible. She'd been kept later at school than usual, and although it was already March, the sky was overcast, it was beginning to get dark, and a fine drizzling rain made the pavements slippery. Togo was in a worse mood than usual. He had slouched along, stopping for whole minutes at lampposts and dustbins and misbehaving extravagantly in the most inconvenient places, in spite of her frantic tugs at the leash to try to get him off the pavement. He was too strong for her to control, and he knew it. She almost believed that he had a spite against her, and enjoyed showing that he didn't have to do anything she wanted, as if it wasn't bad enough having to go out in public with an animal so unkempt and anti-social.

They reached the zebra crossing on the hill. The traffic was moving fast, as it always did during the evening rush-hour. She would have to wait for a break before she could step off the pavement, especially as, in the half dark, she knew from her

Dad's comments when he was driving, pedestrians on the road were not easy to see. She stood still and dragged at Togo's lead. But Togo did not mean to be dictated to by a little school-girl, and after a moment's hesitation, he pulled too. He was off, into the middle of the on-coming traffic, wrenching at the leash, which she had twisted round her hand in order to get a better grip. She threw all her weight against his, but she was no match for him. She thought she felt the worn leather snap, she heard the sound of screaming brakes and someone shouted. She had time to think, 'What am I going to say to Mrs Matthews?', before her head swam and she thought she was going to faint.

She found herself standing on the further side of the road. She saw a huddle of people, surrounding stationary cars. Two drivers had left their vehicles and were abusing each other. As the crowd swayed, she saw the bonnet of a red car crumpled by its contact with the back of a large yellow van. She saw, too, a dark stain on the road surface. Blood. Blood made her feel sick, and her head swam again. She hesitated, knowing that she ought to go among the watching people to make herself look, perhaps to try to explain how Togo had pulled, how she hadn't been strong enough to hold him back. Someone should be told whose dog he was. Someone would have to go and break the terrible news to Mrs Matthews.

As she was considering this, she heard the siren of a police car and the two-note call of an ambulance. She thought, 'Perhaps someone got badly hurt in one of the cars, and it's all my fault.' Her courage evaporated, and she turned away from the accident and began to walk, on legs that trembled, up the hill towards her own home. She thought, 'I'll go and tell Mum.' But then she remembered how much Mrs Matthews loved horrible Togo, how she talked about him as her only friend, and how dreadful it was going to be for her to open her front door to find a policeman telling her that her dog was dead. Besides, the policeman might say that it was all her, the girl's, fault. She had to go first to Mrs Matthews' house, to break the news gently, and also to explain that she had tried her best to prevent the accident.

She found that she must have been walking really fast,

which was surprising, considering how much she was dreading the ordeal in front of her. She had reached the grocer's and the newspaper shop at the top of the High Street almost before she'd realized. She saw Sybil Grainger coming out of the newspaper shop, and she was ready to say, 'Hi!' and to pretend that there was nothing wrong, but luckily Sybil seemed not to have seen her. She turned the corner into Grange Road, relieved that she hadn't had to carry on a conversation. Grange Road also seemed shorter than usual; now she had to go along Fenton Crescent till she reached the small side street where Mrs Matthews lived, in one of the row of little old cottages known as Paradise Row.

Her heart beat furiously as she unlatched the small wooden gate and walked the short distance up to the front door, rehearsing exactly how to say what she had to. She lifted the knocker. As it came down on the wood, it made a hollow, echoing sound.

Extraordinary. From the other side of the door, she heard something very much like Togo's deep, menacing growl. She must be in such a state of nerves that she was imagining impossible things. Or perhaps when she felt faint out there in the road, she had fallen and hit her head and been concussed. She felt her scalp, under the straight, silky hair, but she couldn't find any tender spots. She waited. Mrs Matthews was arthritic and always took a long time to answer the door, and there was no hurry for the message she was going to receive.

Steps came slowly, dragging a little, along the passage. The door opened, and she braced herself for the shock she was about to administer and the scolding she was certainly going to receive.

But when Mrs Matthews looked out, she behaved in a very peculiar way. Instead of saying immediately, 'Where's Togo?' she asked nothing of her visitor, but bent forward and peered out, looking up and down the short row of cottages, as if she were searching for something or someone who might be coming or going in the street. Her head with its thinning grey hair was so close that the girl stepped back, opening her mouth to begin her explanation. But what she saw in the passage behind the old woman stopped her from uttering a sound.

At the further end of the passage was a dog. Togo. Togo, whole, apparently unharmed, his collar round his neck, and the end of the broken leash still attached, dragging behind him.

For a moment she thought he was going to spring forward and attack her. Then she saw that, instead, he was backing, shrinking as far away as he could get. He was making a curious noise, not a howl, nor a growl, but a sort of whine. She noticed that he was trembling. She had never seen Togo tremble before. He was showing whites round his yellow eyes and the short hair round his muzzle was bristling.

She started to speak. But Mrs Matthews appeared not to have heard her. She was turning back to calm the terrified dog. She was saying, 'Whatever's the matter with you, Togo? Think you're seeing a ghost?'

GORDON R. DICKSON

Computers
Don't Argue

Treasure Book Club

PLEASE DO NOT FOLD, SPINDLE
OR MUTILATE THIS CARD

Mr: Walter A. Child Balance: $4.98
Dear Customer: Enclosed is your latest book selection. 'Kid-napped', by Robert Louis Stevenson.

437 Woodlawn Drive
Panduk, Michigan
Nov. 16, 1965

Treasure Book Club
1823 Mandy Street
Chicago, Illinois

Dear Sirs:
I wrote you recently about the computer punch card you

sent, billing me for 'Kim', by Rudyard Kipling. I did not open the package containing it until I had already mailed you my cheque for the amount on the card. On opening the package, I found the book missing half its pages. I sent it back to you, requesting either another copy or my money back. Instead, you have sent me a copy of 'Kidnapped', by Robert Louis Stevenson. Will you please straighten this out?

I hereby return the copy of 'Kidnapped'.

Sincerely yours,

Walter A. Child

Treasure Book Club
SECOND NOTICE
PLEASE DO NOT FOLD, SPINDLE
OR MUTILATE THIS CARD

Mr: Walter A. Child Balance: $4.98
For 'Kidnapped', by Robert Louis Stevenson
(If remittance has been made for the above, please disregard this notice)

437 Woodlawn Drive
Panduk, Michigan
Jan. 21, 1966

Treasure Book Club
1823 Mandy Street
Chicago, Illinois

Dear Sirs:

May I direct your attention to my letter of November 16, 1965? You are still continuing to dun me with computer punch cards for a book I did not order. Whereas, actually, it is your company that owes *me* money.

Sincerely yours,

Walter A. Child

Treasure Book Club
1823 Mandy Street
Chicago, Illinois
Feb. 1, 1966

Mr. Walter A. Child
437 Woodlawn Drive
Panduk, Michigan

Dear Mr. Child:
We have sent you a number of reminders concerning an amount owing to us as a result of book purchases you have made from us. This amount, which is $4.98 is now long over-due.

This situation is disappointing to us, particularly since there was no hesitation on our part in extending you credit at the time original arrangements for these purchases were made by you. If we do not receive payment in full by return mail, we will be forced to turn the matter over to a collection agency.

Very truly yours,
Samuel P. Grimes
Collection Mgr.

437 Woodlawn Drive
Panduk, Michigan
Feb. 5, 1966

Dear Mr. Grimes:
Will you stop sending me punch cards and form letters and make me some kind of a direct answer from a human being?

I don't owe you money. *You* owe me money. Maybe I should turn your company over to a collection agency.

Walter A. Child

FEDERAL COLLECTION OUTFIT

88 Prince Street
Chicago, Illinois
Feb. 28, 1966

Mr. Walter A. Child
437 Woodlawn Drive
Panduk, Michigan

Dear Mr. Child:
Your account with the Treasure Book Club, of $4.98 plus interest and charges has been turned over to our agency for collection. The amount due is now $6.83. Please send your cheque for this amount or we shall be forced to take immediate action.

Jacob N. Harshe
Vice President

FEDERAL COLLECTION OUTFIT

88 Prince Street
Chicago, Illinois
April 8, 1966

Mr. Walter A. Child
437 Woodlawn Drive
Panduk, Michigan

Dear Mr. Child:
You have seen fit to ignore our courteous requests to settle your long overdue account with Treasure Book Club, which is now, with accumulated interest and charges, in the amount of $7.51.
If payment in full is not forthcoming by April 11, 1966 we will be forced to turn the matter over to our attorneys for immediate court action.

Ezekiel B. Harshe
President

MALONEY, MAHONEY,
MACNAMARA and PRUITT
Attorneys

89 Prince Street
Chicago, Illinois
April 29, 1966

Mr. Walter A. Child
437 Woodlawn Drive
Panduk, Michigan

Dear Mr Child:

Your indebtedness to the Treasure Book Club has been referred to us for legal action to collect.

This indebtedness is now in the amount of $10.01. If you will send us this amount so that we may receive it before May 5, 1966, the matter may be satisfied. However, if we do not receive satisfaction in full by that date, we will take steps to collect through the courts.

I am sure you will see the advantage of avoiding a judgment against you, which as a matter of record would do lasting harm to your credit rating.

Very truly yours,
Hagthorpe M. Pruitt, Jr.
Attorney-at-law

437 Woodlawn Drive
Panduk, Michigan
May 4, 1966

Mr. Hagthorpe M. Pruitt, Jr.
Maloney, Mahoney, MacNamara and Pruitt
89 Prince Street
Chicago, Illinois

Dear Mr. Pruitt:

You don't know what a pleasure it is to me in this matter to get a letter from a live human being to whom I can explain the situation.

The whole matter is silly. I explained it fully in my letters to the Treasure Book Company. But I might as well have been trying to explain to the computer that puts out their punch cards, for all the good it seemed to do. Briefly, what happened was I ordered a copy of 'Kim', by Rudyard Kipling, for $4.98. When I opened the package they sent me, I found the book had only half its pages, but I'd previously mailed a cheque to pay them for the book.

I sent the book back to them, asking either for a whole copy or my money back. Instead, they sent me a copy of 'Kidnapped', by Robert Louis Stevenson—which I had not ordered; and for which they have been trying to collect from me.

Meanwhile, I am still waiting for the money back that they owe me for the copy of 'Kim' that I didn't get. That's the whole story. Maybe you can help me straighten them out.

Relievedly yours,
Walter A. Child

P.S.: I also sent them back their copy of 'Kidnapped', as soon as I got it, but it hasn't seemed to help. They have never even acknowledged getting it back.

MALONEY, MAHONEY,
MACNAMARA and PRUITT
Attorneys

89 Prince Street
Chicago, Illinois
May 9, 1966

Mr. Walter A. Child
437 Woodlawn Drive
Panduk, Michigan

Dear Mr Child:

I am in possession of no information indicating that any item purchased by you from the Treasure Book Club has been returned.

I would hardly think that, if the case had been as you stated, the Treasure Book Club would have retained us to collect the amount owing from you.

If I do not receive your payment in full within three days, by May 12, 1966, we will be forced to take legal action.

Very truly yours,

Hagthorpe M. Pruitt, Jr.

COURT OF MINOR CLAIMS
Chicago, Illinois

Mr. Walter A. Child
437 Woodlawn Drive
Panduk, Michigan

Be informed that a judgment was taken and entered against you in this court this day of May 26, 1966 in the amount of $15.66 including court costs.

Payment in satisfaction of this judgment may be made to this court or to the adjudged creditor. In the case of payment being made to the creditor, a release should be obtained from the creditor and filed with this court in order to free you of legal obligation in connection with this judgment.

Under the recent Reciprocal Claims Act, if you are a citizen of a different state, a duplicate claim may be automatically entered and judged against you in your own state so that collection may be made there as well as in the State of Illinois.

COURT OF MINOR CLAIMS
Chicago, Illinois

PLEASE DO NOT FOLD, SPINDLE
OR MUTILATE THIS CARD

Judgment was passed this day of May 27, 1966, under Statute $15.66

Against: Child, Walter A. of 437 Woodlawn Drive, Panduk, Michigan. Pray to enter a duplicate claim for judgment

In: Picayune Court—Panduk, Michigan

For Amount: Statute 941

437 Woodlawn Drive
Panduk, Michigan
May 31, 1966

Samuel P. Grimes
Vice President, Treasure Book Club
1823 Mandy Street
Chicago, Illinois

Grimes:

This business has gone far enough. I've got to come down to Chicago on business of my own tomorrow. I'll see you then and we'll get this straightened out once and for all, about who owes what to whom, and how much!

Yours,

Walter A. Child

From the desk of the Clerk
Picayune Court

June 1, 1966

Harry:

The attached computer card from Chicago's Minor Claims Court against A. Walter has a 1500-series Statute number on it. That puts it over in Criminal with you, rather than Civil, with me. So I herewith submit it for your computer instead of mine. How's business?

Joe

CRIMINAL RECORDS
Panduk, Michigan

PLEASE DO NOT FOLD, SPINDLE
OR MUTILATE THIS CARD

Convicted: (Child) A. Walter
On: May 26, 1966
Address: 437 Woodlawn Drive
Panduk, Mich.
Crim: Statute: 1566 (Corrected) 1567
Crime: Kidnap
Date: Nov. 16, 1965
Notes: At large. To be picked up at once.

POLICE DEPARTMENT, PANDUK, MICHIGAN, TO POLICE DEPARTMENT CHICAGO, ILLINOIS. CONVICTED SUBJECT A. (COMPLETE FIRST NAME UNKNOWN) WALTER, SOUGHT HERE IN CONNECTION REF. YOUR NOTIFICATION OF JUDGMENT FOR KIDNAP OF CHILD NAMED ROBERT LOUIS STEVENSON, ON NOV. 16, 1965. INFORMATION HERE INDICATES SUBJECT FLED HIS RESIDENCE, AT 437 WOODLAWN DRIVE, PANDUK, AND MAY BE AGAIN IN YOUR AREA.

POSSIBLE CONTACT IN YOUR AREA: THE TREASURE BOOK CLUB, 1823 MANDY STREET, CHICAGO, ILLINOIS. SUBJECT NOT KNOWN TO BE DANGEROUS. PICK UP AND HOLD, ADVISING US OF CAPTURE...

TO POLICE DEPARTMENT, PANDUK, MICHIGAN. REFERENCE YOUR REQUEST TO PICK UP AND HOLD A. (COMPLETE FIRST NAME UNKNOWN) WALTER, WANTED IN PANDUK ON STATUTE 1567, CRIME OF KIDNAPPING.

SUBJECT ARRESTED AT OFFICES OF TREASURE BOOK CLUB, OPERATING THERE UNDER ALIAS WALTER ANTHONY CHILD AND ATTEMPTING TO COLLECT $4.98 FROM ONE SAMUEL P. GRIMES, EMPLOYEE OF THAT COMPANY.

DISPOSAL: HOLDING FOR YOUR ADVICE.

POLICE DEPARTMENT PANDUK, MICHIGAN TO POLICE DEPARTMENT CHICAGO, ILLINOIS.

REF: A. WALTER (ALIAS WALTER ANTHONY CHILD) SUBJECT WANTED FOR CRIME OF KIDNAP, YOUR AREA, REF: YOUR COMPUTER PUNCH CARD NOTIFICATION OF JUDGMENT, DATED MAY 27, 1966. COPY OUR CRIMINAL RECORDS PUNCH CARD HEREWITH FORWARDED TO YOUR COMPUTER SECTION.

CRIMINAL RECORDS
Chicago, Illinois

PLEASE DO NOT FOLD, SPINDLE OR MUTILATE THIS CARD

SUBJECT (CORRECTION—OMITTED RECORD SUPPLIED)
APPLICABLE STATUTE NO. 1567
JUDGMENT NO. 456789
TRIAL RECORD: APPARENTLY MISFILED AND UNAVAILABLE

DIRECTION: TO APPEAR FOR SENTENCING BEFORE JUDGE JOHN ALEXANDER MCDIVOT, COURTROOM A JUNE 9, 1966

From the Desk of
Judge Alexander J. McDivot

June 2, 1966

Dear Tony:

I've got an adjudged criminal coming up before me for sentencing Thursday morning—but the trial transcript is apparently misfiled.

I need some kind of information (Ref: A. Walter—Judgment

No. 456789, Criminal). For example, what about the victim of the kidnapping? Was victim harmed?

Jack McDivot

June 3, 1966

Records Search Unit
Re: Ref: Judgment No. 456789—was victim harmed?

Tonio Malagasi
Records Division

June 3, 1966

To: United States Statistics Office
Attn: Information Section
Subject: Robert Louis Stevenson
Query: Information concerning

Records Search Unit
Criminal Records Division
Police Department
Chicago, Ill.

June 5, 1966

To: Records Search Unit
Criminal Records Division
Police Department
Chicago, Illinois
Subject: Your query re Robert Louis Stevenson (File no. 189623)
Action: Subject deceased. Age at death 44 yrs. Further information requested?

A.K.
Information Section
U.S. Statistics Office

June 6th, 1966

To: United States Statistics Office
Attn.: Information Division
Subject: RE: File no. 189623

No further information required.
Thank you.

Records Search Unit
Criminal Records Division
Police Department
Chicago, Illinois

June 7, 1966

To: Tonio Malagasi
Records Division
Re: Ref: judgment No. 456789—victim is dead.

Records Search Unit

June 7, 1966

To: Judge Alexander J. McDivot's Chambers

Dear Jack:
Ref: Judgement No. 456789. The victim in this kidnap case was apparently slain.

From the strange lack of background information on the killer and his victim, as well as the victim's age, this smells to me like a gangland killing. This for your information. Don't quote me. It seems to me, though, that Stevenson—the victim—has a name that rings a faint bell with me. Possibly, one of the East Coast Mob, since the association comes back to me as something about pirates—possibly New York dockage hijackers—and something about buried loot.

As I say, above is only speculation for your private gui-

dance.
　　Any time I can help...

Best,

Tony Malagasi
Records Division

MICHAEL R. REYNOLDS
Attorney-at-law

49 Water Street
Chicago, Illinois

June 8, 1966

Dear Tim:
　　Regrets: I can't make the fishing trip. I've been court-appointed here to represent a man about to be sentenced tomorrow on a kidnapping charge.
　　Ordinarily, I might have tried to beg off, and McDivot, who is doing the sentencing, would probably have turned me loose. But this is the damndest thing you ever heard of.
　　The man being sentenced has apparently been not only charged, but adjudged guilty as a result of a comedy of errors too long to go into here. He not only isn't guilty—he's got the best case I ever heard of for damages against one of the larger Book Clubs headquartered here in Chicago. And that's a case I wouldn't mind taking on.
　　It's inconceivable—but damnably possible, once you stop to think of it in this day and age of machine-made records—that a completely innocent man could be put in this position.
　　There shouldn't be much to it. I've asked to see McDivot tomorrow before the time for sentencing, and it'll just be a matter of explaining to him. Then I can discuss the damage suit with my freed client at his leisure.
　　Fishing next weekend?

Yours,

Mike

MICHAEL R. REYNOLDS
Attorney-at-law

49 Water Street
Chicago, Illinois
June 10

Dear Tim:

In haste—

No fishing this coming week either. Sorry.

You won't believe it. My innocent-as-a-lamb-and-I'm-not-kidding client has just been sentenced to death for first-degree murder in connection with the death of his kidnap victim.

Yes, I explained the whole thing to McDivot. And when he explained his situation to me, I nearly fell out of my chair.

It wasn't a matter of my not convincing him. It took less than three minutes to show him that my client should never have been within the walls of the County Jail for a second. But—get this—McDivot couldn't do a thing about it.

The point is, my man had already been judged guilty according to the computerised records. In the absence of a trial record—of course there never was one (but that's something I'm not free to explain to you now)—the judge has to go by what records are available. And in the case of an adjudged prisoner, McDivot's only legal choice was whether to sentence to life imprisonment, or execution.

The death of the kidnap victim, according to the statute, made the death penalty mandatory. Under the new laws governing length of time for appeal, which has been shortened because of the new system of computerising records, to force an elimination of unfair delay and mental anguish to those condemned, I have five days in which to file an appeal, and ten to have it acted on.

Needless to say, I am not going to monkey with an appeal. I'm going directly to the Governor for a pardon—after which we will get this farce reversed. McDivot has already written the governor, also, explaining that his sentence was ridiculous, but that he had no choice. Between the two of us, we ought to have a pardon in short order.

Then, I'll make the fur fly …

And we'll get in some fishing.

Best,

Mike

OFFICE OF THE
GOVERNOR OF ILLINOIS

June 17, 1966

Mr. Michael R. Reynolds
49 Water Street
Chicago, Illinois

Dear Mr. Reynolds:

In reply to your query about the request for pardon for Walter A. Child (A. Walter), may I inform you that the Governor is still on his trip with the Midwest Governors Committee, examining the Wall in Berlin. He should be back next Friday.

I will bring your request and letters to his attention the minute he returns.

Very truly yours,

Clara B. Jilks
Secretary to the Governor

June 27, 1966

Michael R. Reynolds
49 Water Street
Chicago, Illinois

Dear Mike:

Where is that pardon?

My execution date is only five days from now!

Walt

June 29, 1966

Walter A. Child (A. Walter)
Cell Block E
Illinois State Penitentiary
Joliet, Illinois

Dear Walt:

The Governor returned, but was called away immediately to the White House in Washington to give his views on interstate sewage.

I am camping on his doorstep and will be on him the moment he arrives here.

Meanwhile, I agree with you about the seriousness of the situation. The warden at the prison there, Mr. Allen Magruder, will bring this letter to you and have a private talk with you. I urge you to listen to what he has to say; and I enclose letters from your family also urging you to listen to Warden Magruder.

Yours,

Mike

June 30, 1966

Michael R. Reynolds
49 Water Street
Chicago, Illinois

Dear Mike: (This letter being smuggled out by Warden Magruder)

As I was talking to Warden Magruder in my cell, here, news was brought to him that the Governor has at last returned for a while to Illinois, and will be in his office early tomorrow morning, Friday. So you will have time to get the pardon signed by him and delivered to the prison in time to stop my execution on Saturday.

Accordingly, I have turned down the Warden's kind offer of a chance to escape; since he told me he could by no means guarantee to have all the guards out of my way when I tried it;

and there was a chance of my being killed escaping.

But now everything will straighten itself out. Actually, an experience as fantastic as this had to break down sometime under its own weight.

Best,

Walt

FOR THE SOVEREIGN
STATE OF ILLINOIS

I, Hubert Daniel Willikens, Governor of the State of Illinois, and invested with the authority and powers appertaining thereto, including the power to pardon those in my judgment wrongfully convicted or otherwise deserving of executive mercy, do this day of July 1, 1966 announce and proclaim that Walter A. Child (A. Walter) now in custody as a consequence of erroneous conviction upon a crime of which he is entirely innocent, is fully and freely pardoned of the said crime. And I do direct the necessary authorities having custody of the said Walter A. Child (A. Walter) in whatever place or places he may be held, to immediately free, release, and allow unhindered departure to him...

Interdepartmental Routing Service

PLEASE DO NOT FOLD, MUTILATE,
OR SPINDLE THIS CARD

Failure to route Document properly.

To: Governor Hubert Daniel Willikens
Re: Pardon issued to Walter A. Child, July 1, 1966

Dear State Employee:
    You have failed to attach your Routing Number.

PLEASE: Resubmit document with this card and form 876, explaining your authority for placing a TOP RUSH category on this document. Form 876 must be signed by your Department Superior.

RESUBMIT ON: Earliest possible date ROUTING SERVICE office is open. In this case, Tuesday, July 5, 1966.

WARNING: Failure to submit form 876 WITH THE SIGNATURE OF YOUR SUPERIOR may make you liable to prosecution for misusing a Service of the State Government. A warrant may be issued for your arrest.

There are NO exceptions. YOU have been WARNED.

Harold Rolseth

*H*ey You Down There!

Calvin Spender drained his coffee cup and wiped his mouth with the back of his hand. He burped loudly and then proceeded to fill a corncob pipe with coarsely shredded tobacco. He scratched a match across the top of the table and holding it to his pipe, he sucked noisily until billows of acrid smoke poured from his mouth.

Dora Spender sat across the table from her husband, her breakfast scarcely touched. She coughed lightly, and then, as no frown appeared on Calvin's brow, she said, 'Are you going to dig in the well this morning, Calvin?'

Calvin fixed his small red-rimmed eyes upon her, and as if she had not spoken, said, 'Git going at the chores right away. You're going to be hauling up dirt.'

'Yes, Calvin,' Dora whispered. Calvin cleared his throat, and the action caused his Adam's apple to move rapidly under the loose red skin on his neck. He rose from the table and went out of the kitchen door, kicking viciously at the tawny cat which had been lying on the doorstep.

Dora gazed at him and wondered for the thousandth time what it was that Calvin reminded her of. It was not some other person. It was something else. Sometimes it seemed as though the answer was about to spring to her mind, as just now when Calvin had cleared his throat. But always it stopped just short of her consciousness. It was disturbing to know with such certainty that Calvin looked like something other than himself and yet not know what that something was. Some day though, Dora knew, the answer would come to her. She rose hurriedly from the table and set about her chores.

Halfway between the house and the barn, a doughnut-shaped mound of earth surrounded a hole. Calvin went to the edge of the hole and stared down into it distastefully. Only necessity could have forced him to tackle this task, but it was either this digging or the hauling of barrels and barrels of water each day from Nord Fisher's farm half a mile down the road.

Calvin's herd of scrub cattle was small, but the amount of water it drank was astonishing. For two weeks now, ever since his well had gone dry, Calvin had been hauling water, and the disagreeable chore was becoming more unpleasant because of neighbour Nord's hints that some kind of payment for the water would only be fair.

Several feet back from the edge of the hole, Calvin had driven a heavy iron stake into the ground, and to this was attached a crude rope ladder. The rope ladder had become necessary when the hole had reached a depth well beyond the length of any wooden ladder Calvin owned.

Calvin hoped desperately that he would not have to go much further. He estimated that he was now down fifty or sixty feet, a common depth for many wells in the area. His greatest fear was that he would hit a layer of rock which would call for the services of a well-drilling outfit. Both his funds and his credit-rating were far too low for such a team.

Calvin picked up a bucket to which was attached a long rope and lowered it into the hole. It was Dora's backbreaking task to pull the bucket hand over hand after Calvin had filled it from the bottom of the hole. With a mumbled curse, Calvin emptied his pipe and started down the rope ladder. By the time he got to the bottom of the hole and had filled the bucket, Dora should be there to haul it up. If she weren't, she would hear about it.

From the house, Dora saw Calvin prepare to enter the well and she worked with desperate haste to complete her chores. She reached the hole just as a muffled shout from below indicated that the bucket was full.

Summoning all her strength, Dora hauled the bucket up. She emptied it and then lowered it into the hole again. While she waited for the second bucketload, she examined the contents of the first. She was disappointed to find it had only the normal moistness of underground earth. No water seeped from it.

In her own way, Dora was deeply religious and at each tenth bucket she pulled up she murmured an urgent prayer that it would contain more water in it than earth. She had settled at praying at every tenth bucketload because she did not believe it in good taste to pester God with every bucket. Also, she varied the wording of each prayer, feeling that God must become bored with the same plea repeated over and over.

On this particular morning as she lowered the bucket for its tenth loading, she prayed, 'Please God, let something happen this time... let something really and truly happen so I won't have to haul up any more dirt.'

Something happened almost immediately. As the rope slackened in her hands indicating that the bucket had reached the bottom, a scream of sheer terror came up from the hole, and the rope ladder jerked violently. Whimpering sounds of mortal fear sounded faintly, and the ladder grew taut with heavy strain.

Dora fell to her knees and peered down into the darkness. 'Calvin,' she called, 'are you all right? What is it?'

Then with startling suddenness, Calvin appeared. At first Dora was not sure it *was* Calvin. The usual redness of his face was gone; now it was a yellowish green. He was trembling violently and had trouble breathing.

'It must have been a heart attack,' Dora thought, and tried hard to control the surge of joy that came over her.

Calvin lay upon the ground, panting. Finally he gained control of himself. Under ordinary circumstances, Calvin did not converse with Dora but now he seemed eager to talk. 'You know what happened down there?' he said in a shaky voice.

'You know what happened? The complete bottom dropped right out of the hole. All of a sudden it went, and there I was, standing on nothing but air. If I hadn't grabbed a hold of the last rung of the ladder… Why, that hole must be a thousand feet the way the bottom dropped out of it!'

Calvin babbled on, but Dora didn't listen. She was amazed at the remarkable way in which her prayer had been answered. If the hole had no more bottom, there would be no more dirt to haul up.

When Calvin had regained his strength, he crept to the edge of the hole and peered down.

'What are you going to do, Calvin?' Dora asked timidly.

'Do? I'm going to find out how far down that hole goes. Get the flashlight from the kitchen.'

Dora hurried off. When she returned, Calvin had a large ball of binder twine he had brought from the tool shed.

He tied the flashlight securely to the end of the line, switched it on and lowered it into the hole. He paid out the line for about a hundred feet and then stopped. The light was only a feeble glimmer down below and revealed nothing. Calvin lowered the light another hundred feet and this time it was only a twinkling speck as it swung at the end of the line. Calvin released another long length of twine and another and another and now the light was no longer visible, and the large ball of twine had shrunk to a small tangle.

'Almost a full thousand feet,' he whispered in awe. 'And no bottom yet. Might as well pull it up.'

But the line did not come up with Calvin's pull. It stretched and grew taut, but it did not yield to his tugging.

'Must be caught on something,' Calvin muttered, and gave the line a sharp jerk. In reply there was a downward jerk that almost tore the line from his hands.

'Hey!' yelled Calvin. 'The line…it jerked!'

'But, Calvin –' Dora protested.

'Don't Calvin me. I tell you there's something on the end of this line.'

He gave another tug, and again the line was almost pulled from his hands. He tied the line to the stake and sat down to ponder the matter.

'It don't make sense,' he said, more to himself than to Dora. 'What could be down underground a good thousand feet?'

Tentatively he reached and pulled lightly on the line. This time there was no response, and rapidly he began hauling it up. When the end of the line came into view, there was a small white pouch of a leatherlike substance.

Calvin opened the pouch with trembling fingers and shook into his palm a bar of yellow metal and a folded piece of parchment. The bar of metal was not large but it seemed heavy for its size. Calvin got out his jack-knife and scratched the point of the blade across the metal. The knife blade bit into it easily.

'Gold,' said Calvin, his voice shaky. 'Must be a whole pound of it...and just for a measly flashlight. They must be crazy down there.'

He thrust the gold bar into his pocket and opened the small piece of parchment. One side was closely covered with a fine writing. Calvin turned it this way and that and then tossed it on the ground.

'Foreigners,' he said. 'No wonder they ain't got any sense. But it's plain they need flashlights.'

'But, Calvin,' said Dora. 'How could they get down there? There ain't any mines in this part of the country.'

'Ain't you ever heard of them secret government projects?' asked Calvin scornfully. 'This must be one of them. Now I'm going to town to get me a load of flashlights. They must need them bad. Now, mind you watch that hole good. Don't let no one go near it.'

Calvin strode to the battered truck which was standing near the barn and a minute later was rattling down the highway towards Harmony Junction.

Dora picked up the bit of parchment which Calvin had thrown away. She could make nothing of the writing on it. It was all very strange. If it were some secret government undertaking, why would foreigners be taking part? And why would they need flashlights so urgently as to pay a fortune for one?

Suddenly it occurred to her that possibly the people down below didn't know there were English-speaking people up above. She hurried into the house and rummaged through Calvin's rickety desk for paper and pencil. In her search she found a small, ragged dictionary, and she took this with her to the kitchen table. Spelling didn't come easily to Dora.

Her note was a series of questions. Why were they down there? Who were they? Why did they pay so much for an old flashlight?

As she started for the well it occurred to her that possibly the people down there might be hungry. She went back to the kitchen and wrapped a loaf of bread and a fair-sized piece of ham in a clean dish-towel. She added a PS to her note apologizing for the fact that she had nothing better to offer them. Then the thought came to her that since the people down below were obviously foreigners and possibly not too well versed in English, the small dicitionary might be of help to them in answering her note. She wrapped the dictionary with the food in the towel.

It took Dora a long time to lower the bucket, but finally the twine grew slack in her hands and she knew the bucket had reached the bottom. She waited for a few moments and then tugged the line gently. The line held firm below, and Dora seated herself on the mound of earth to wait.

The warm sunlight felt good on her back and it was pleasant to sit and do nothing. She had no fear that Calvin would return soon. She knew that nothing on earth – or under it – could keep Calvin from visiting a number of bars once he was in town, and that with each tavern visited, time would become more and more meaningless to him. She doubted that he would return before morning.

After half an hour Dora gave the line a questioning tug, but it did not yield. She did not mind. It was seldom that she had time to idle away. Usually when Calvin went to town, he burdened her with chores that were to be done during his absence, coupling each order with a threat of what awaited her should his instructions not be carried out.

Dora waited another half hour before tugging at the line again. This time there was a sharp answering jerk, and Dora began hauling the bucket upward. It seemed much heavier now, and twice she had to pause for a rest. When the bucket reached the surface, she saw why it was heavier.

'My goodness,' she murmured as she viewed the dozen or

so yellow metal bars in the bucket. 'They must be real hungry down there!'

A sheet of the strange parchment was also in the bucket, and Dora picked it out expecting to see the strange writing of the first note.

'Well, I declare,' she said when she saw that the note was in English. It was in the same print as the dictionary, and each letter had been made with meticulous care.

She read the note slowly, shaping each word with her lips as she read.

> Your language is barbaric, but the crude code book you sent down made it easy for our scholars to decipher it. We, too, wonder about you. How have you overcome the problem of living in the deadly light? Our legends tell of a race dwelling on the surface but intelligent reasoning has made us ridicule these old tales until now. We would still doubt that you are surface-dwellers except for the fact that our instruments show without question that the opening above us leads to the deadly light.
>
> The clumsy death ray which you sent us indicates that your scientific development is very low. Other than as an object from another race it has no value to us. We sent gold as a courtesy payment only.
>
> The food you call bread is not acceptable to our digestive systems, but the ham is beyond price. It is obviously the flesh of some creature, and we will exchange a double weight of gold for all that you can send us. Send more immediately. Also send a concise history of your race and arrange for your best scientists, such as they are, to communicate with us.
>
> Glar, the Master

'Land sakes,' said Dora. 'Real bossy they are. I've a good mind not to send them anything. I don't dare send them more ham. Calvin would notice if any more is gone.'

Dora took the gold bars to her petunia bed beside the house and buried them in the loose black soil. She paid no heed to the sound of a car coming down the highway at high speed until it passed the house and a wild squawking sounded above the roar of the motor. She hurried around to the front of the house, knowing already what had happened. She stared in dismay at the four chickens which lay dead in the road. She knew that Calvin would blame her and beat her into unconsciousness.

Fear sharpened her wits. Perhaps if she could dispose of the bodies, Calvin would think foxes had got them. Hastily she gathered up the dead chickens and feathers which lay scattered about. When she was finished, there was no evidence of the disaster.

She carried the chickens to the back of the house wondering how she could best dispose of them. Suddenly, as she glanced towards the hole, the answer came to her.

An hour later the four chickens were dressed and neatly cut up. Ignoring the other instructions in the note, she sent the bulky parcel of chicken down into the hole.

She sat down again to enjoy the luxury of doing nothing. When, an hour later, she picked up the line, there was an immediate response from below. The bucket was exceedingly heavy this time, and she was fearful that the line might break. She was dizzy with fatigue when she finally hauled the bucket over to the edge of the hole. This time there were several dozen bars of gold in it and a brief note in the same precise lettering as before.

Our scientists are of the opinion that the flesh you sent down is that of a creature you call chicken. This is the supreme food. Never have we eaten anything so delicious. To show our appreciation we are sending you a bonus payment. Your code book indicates that there is a larger creature similar to chicken called turkey. Send us turkey immediately. I repeat, send us turkey immediately.

Glar, the Master.

'Land sakes,' gasped Dora. 'They must have eaten that chicken raw. Now where in tarnation would I get a turkey?'

She buried the gold bars in another part of her petunia bed. Calvin returned about ten o'clock the next morning. His eyes

73

were bloodshot and his face was a mottled red. The loose folds of skin on his neck hung lower than usual and more than ever he reminded Dora of something that she couldn't quite put a name to.

Calvin stepped down from the truck and Dora cringed, but he seemed too tired and preoccupied to bother with her. He surveyed the hole glumly, then got into the truck and backed it to the edge of the mound of earth. On the back of the truck was a winch with a large drum of steel cable.

'Fix me something to eat,' he ordered Dora.

Dora hurried into the house and began preparing ham and eggs. Each moment she expected Calvin to come in and demand to know, with a few blows, what was holding up his meal. But Calvin seemed very busy in the vicinity of the hole. When Dora went out to call him to eat, she found he had done a surprising amount of work. He had attached an oil drum to the steel cable. This hung over a heavy steel rod which rested across the hole. Stakes driven into the ground on each side of the hole held the rod in place.

'Your breakfast is ready, Calvin,' said Dora.

'Shut up,' Calvin answered.

The winch was driven by an electric motor, and Calvin ran a cable from the motor to an electric outlet on the yard light-post. From the cab he took a number of boxes and placed them in the oil-drum.

'A whole hundred of them,' he chuckled, more to himself than to Dora. 'Fifty-nine cents apiece. Peanuts...one bar of gold will buy thousands.'

Calvin threw the switch which controlled the winch, and with sickening force Dora realized the terrible thing that would soon happen. The creatures down below had no use or regard for flashlights.

Down went the oil drum, the cable screeching shrilly as it passed over the rod above the hole. Calvin got an oil can from the truck and applied oil generously to the rod and cable. In a very short while the cable went slack and Calvin stopped the winch.

'I'll give them an hour to load up the gold,' he said and went to the kitchen for his delayed breakfast.

Dora was almost numb with fear. What would happen when the flashlights came back up, with an insulting note in English, was too horrible to contemplate. Calvin would learn about the gold she had received and very likely kill her.

Calvin ate his breakfast leisurely. Dora busied herself with household tasks, trying with all her might to cast out of her mind the terrible thing which was soon to happen.

Finally Calvin glanced at the wall clock, yawned widely, and tapped out his pipe. Ignoring Dora, he went out to the hole. In spite of her terrible fear, Dora could not resist following him. It was as if some power outside herself forced her to go.

The winch was already reeling the cable when she got to the hole. It seemed only seconds before the oil drum was up. The grin on Calvin's face was broad as he reached out over the hole and dragged the drum to the edge. A look of utter disbelief replaced the grin as he looked into it. His Adam's apple seemed to vibrate under his red-skinned throat, and once again part of Dora's mind tried to recall what it was that Calvin reminded her of.

Calvin was making flat, bawling sounds like a lost calf. He hauled the drum out of the hole and dumped its contents on the ground. The flashlights, many of them dented and with lenses broken, made a sizeable pile.

With a tremendous kick Calvin sent flashlights flying in all directions. One, with a note attached, landed at Dora's feet. Either Calvin was so blinded by rage that he didn't see it, or he assumed it was written in the same unreadable script as the first note.

'You down there!' he screamed into the hole. 'You filthy swine! I'll fix you. I'll make you sorry you ever double-crossed me. I'll... I'll...'

He dashed for the house and Dora hastily snatched up the note.

You are even more stupid than we thought. Your clumsy death rays are useless to us. We informed you of this. We want turkey. Send us turkey immediately.

Glar, the Master.

She crumpled the note swiftly as Calvin came from the house with his double-barrelled shotgun. For a moment, Dora thought that he knew everything and was about to kill her.

'Please, Calvin,' she said.

'Shut up,' said Calvin. 'You saw me work the winch. Can you do it?'

'Why, yes, but what...?'

'Listen, you stupid cow. I'm going down there to fix those dirty foreigners. You send me down and bring me up.' He seized Dora by the shoulder. 'And if you mess things up, I'll fix you too! I'll really and truly fix you.'

Dora nodded dumbly.

Calvin put his gun in the oil drum and pushed it to the centre of the hole. Then, hanging on to the cable, he carefully lowered himself into the drum.

'Give me just one hour to run those dirty rats down, then bring me back up,' he said.

Dora threw the switch and the oil drum went down. When the cable slackened, she stopped the winch. She spent most of the next hour praying that Calvin would not find the people down there and become a murderer.

Exactly an hour later, Dora started the oil drum upward. The motor laboured mightily as though under a tremendous strain, and the cable seemed stretched almost to breaking point.

Dora gasped when the oil drum came into view. Calvin was not in it! She shut off the motor and hastened to the drum, half expecting to find Calvin crouching down inside. But Calvin was not there. Instead there were scores of gold bars and on top of them a sheet of the familiar white parchment.

'Land sakes,' Dora said, as she took in a full view of the drum's contents. She had no idea of the value of the treasure upon which she gazed. She only knew it must be immense. Carefully, she reached down and picked out the note, which she read in her slow, precise way.

Not even the exquisite flavour of the chicken compares to the incomparable goodness of the live turkey you sent down to us. We must confess that we thought turkey would be rather different from this, but this does not matter. So delicious was the turkey that we are again sending you a bonus payment. We beg you to send us more turkey immediately.

Glar, the Master

Dora read the note a second time to make sure she understood it fully. 'Well, I declare,' she said in considerable wonder. 'I do declare'.

DAVID HARMER
Out On The Wire

Mud stuck to his face, clogging his mouth. Shielding his head with an upturned helmet, he gasped for breath. The mud squeezed around his skull, stopping his eyes, his ears.

Early light began to rub away at the sky. Soon he could see where quiet farms and undisturbed woods had twisted into a ruptured landscape of craters, the stumps of trees jabbing through thick curls of wire.

Mud. Holes. Wire. Bodies. Many many bodies.

He gently moved his shoulders, then screamed as the wire dug deeper, wrapping around sinew and muscle. More shells exploded and the burning air kicked into him. He burrowed into the mud, leaving just a splinter of mouth free.

All night the men in their trenches had heard him. By daylight the body was clearly visible, snarled up in the barbed wire.

A good officer. A capable, well trained man. He had taken out his patrol without a hint of anxiety into severe enemy fire. Went to a good school of course. Public Schools Rugby Captain 1909–10. Played Sandhurst. Won a most honourable draw.

Even so, there had been private defeat. One tackle had knocked the breath right out of him. He scrabbled for air, leaving his face open and vulnerable. An opponent kicked him hard as though driving for touch. His mouth had burst open. He had pressed his face hard into the playing field to staunch the blood.

Back at Church House the entire school and staff had applauded. His back was as sore as his swollen face from hands slapping him. By the time he got to the stage he was almost crying.

'I say Roundtree,' the Head looked down, 'don't blub. Play the man sir, play the man.'

Gunfire clattered like quick applause, chattering fiercely over the mud. He had strength enough to push deeper behind the helmet.

> The Grove Nursing Home,
> Market Lane,
> Ashburton-cum-Downham,
> Nr. Sevenoaks
> Kent
> 1.2.20

Dear Mr. Clarke,

Thank you so much for writing to me in connection with our patient, Mr. Edward Roundtree. I am delighted to learn of your interest in his application for the post of French master at Sydenham Boys Grammar School.

I will certainly furnish you with all the medical and academic records for which you asked.

Mr. Roundtree, although still clearly marked from his terrible injuries, possesses a clear and lucid intelligence as well as an excellent degree in French. He is also fluent in Italian, German and has a smattering of Dutch.

He couples this academic prowess with a friendly manner and an earnest desire for hard work. Although often in pain still, I can assure you that he is in good spirit and would certainly be capable of fulfilling the requirements of the post. He could take up his position later in the year when he will be discharged from my care.

Yours sincerely,

P.R. Bolton-Gould, M.D., F.R.C.S., J.P.

Of course they called him Punch. He didn't expect much more from the boys than this accurate cruelty.

With his stooped back and curious hobble, Punch he became, stumping around the corridors with great determination, giving lessons in faultless French and gradually acquiring the skills of his new trade.

On the whole the boys responded well. Many had lost fathers, brothers, uncles in the same battlefields that had twisted his back. The school now remembered old boys and masters who had perished, their names recorded in a large book and mentioned in prayers. Besides, however much his body was crippled, Punch's intellect remained keen and clear. The face, with brown eyes and neatly trimmed moustache, demanded and won respect.

Atkinson, though, accorded him none. It was partly to do with Atkinson's lack of aptitude with languages and partly to do with his natural inclination to bully. A big, red-faced boy who, even in his earlier years in the school, made obvious his contempt and dislike.

'Atkinson. Please conjugate the verb être, to be.'

'Je suis.......Punch,

Tu es......Punch,

Il est......PUNCH!'

A minor unpleasantness that was soon dealt with, but a shot that found its mark for all that. It was not repeated that lesson. Atkinson rarely followed up his attacks. Content with the wounding, he waited until more opportunities presented themselves, which over the years, they did with regularity.

'You're late for my lesson Atkinson. Why?'

'Rugger practice sir.'

'I see. But your colleagues came in ten minutes ago.'

'Extra practice sir. Mr Sloane wanted me to practice my kicking sir. Vital element to the game sir.'

'So I understand Atkinson.'

'Really sir? Didn't think you played much rugger these days

sir, bearing in mind your condition.'

All of this was conducted in lowered voices outside the classroom. The corridor was empty, the confrontation unwitnessed. Certainly Punch could have hit the boy, gaining only sympathy and understanding from parents and colleagues alike. This was not his way though, especially with a boy of fifteen. Punch was in no mood for violence then or ever. Indeed, he had never been known to hit any boy. Punch was, in all senses, a pacifist.

'Atkinson, your wit exceeds your taste. It most certainly does. Get inside the room boy.'

That evening the shelling stopped. A stretcher party was mustered and they clambered out to where he lay. Although a lot of the wire was embedded in his back, shoulders and chest, his legs were free. This was great luck. Broken legs might mend. The damaged back would never straighten but at least he might walk one day.

Atkinson worked through the school like splinters of shrapnel pushing through Punch's body. The ache in his back was inflamed by constant contact with the boy, whose years at the school did nothing to moderate his opinions.

'I wonder Atkinson why your father wishes you to stay and move up to the sixth. Your attitude to this school and its staff scarcely endorses such an action.'

'He wants me to learn more and grow wise like you Punch; it keeps him happy. It doesn't matter one way or the other; sooner or later I'll take on the business. I'll have it all one day.'

'Good. You may well be happier as a butcher Atkinson. Certainly further studies of French are not to be recommended. Molière, Racine and Voltaire are unlikely to be sources of great illumination to you are they? Indeed, I......'

'For God's sake shut up Punch! Why are you always droning on about the bloody French? My father says they ran like mad from their trenches. Mon Dieu! Mon Dieu!' This part of the outburst was accompanied by wild gestures and an absurdly exaggerated accent, 'A pack of garlic-eating yellow bellies, the lot of them. My father says they were as bad as the Germans for running away. Mon Dieu!'

Only the unexpected and unpredictable reaction of Punch could have shocked the class more than this display of Atkinson at his boldest and most offensive. The teacher moved with extraordinary agility and speed. Atkinson cried out as Punch pulled down his head, fingers locked in the thick, yellow hair.

'What do you know?' he yelled. 'What? Of any of it? What?'

Slowly Punch's anger left him. It was ridiculous to let the spite of a boy intimidate him. The pain in his back intensified. He released the boy's hair and spoke softly to the scarlet, panting face.

'If we learn, slowly, carefully, the languages of others, the French, the Germans, the Italians. If we learn these languages then perhaps we can grow to understand these people. To see them more like us. To know our differences, our similarities. And then Atkinson, perhaps we shan't want to make war on them.'

The years continued, the back as distorted as ever, the walk as grotesque. Daily discomfort and pain dulled to a manageable routine of shopping, visits to hospital, to Church House for the rugby, to Folkstone to visit his parents and increasingly, an involvement with local Pacifist organisations.

During these years Punch took on a variety of private pupils, often adults who wished to improve their conversational languages. So it was that in the autumn of 1938, soon after his forty-fifth birthday, Punch met Janet Byron.

She came, she said, to improve her hopelessly inadequate schoolgirl French. An attractive girl with a job in a busy Sydenham office, she arrived for an hour's lesson each Thursday evening. This soon became the centre of his week. Despite all his resolve and harshly realistic self-appraisal, he knew he was being drawn towards her.

She was of course much younger than Punch, twenty-one or two with long auburn hair and grey eyes. She spent a lot of time and money on her appearance and always arrived at his home punctually, looking composed and elegant.

Punch grew increasingly dependant on these meetings. If she ever missed one his week was ruined. This was rare though. Janet appeared to enjoy his company and soon proved an excellent pupil.

After she had gone he could still feel her warmth fill the room, almost touch the shape of her beside him. He would begin long and involved conversations. He would explain that he fully understood that a girl of her looks and style would scarcely find a cripple attractive but that there was certainly such a thing as two intellects meeting. Such relationships were possible.

Of course he said nothing of this when she came to her next lesson but inevitably the physical distances between them decreased. The necessary closeness of the teacher and the taught was a little more emphasised. Hands were brushed, legs came slightly into contact.

Later he would wish he'd said more or torment himself with guilt remembering the accidental touch of her arm, the less accidental touch of her hair as they bent over guidebooks and maps together.

He began to nurture more candid dreams. Now she laughed and said how much she admired him, his strength, his struggle against pain. How, despite everything, she did find him attractive. How she knew she could easily forget his poor back. How much she wanted his agile fingers through her hair. Would he kiss her? Would he slip off her dress and kiss her? Would he?

'I thought I might begin to learn Italian soon, Ted. Do you think I might?'

She was sitting at his desk drinking a glass of wine. He watched her carefully. She had missed several lessons recently, giving no special reason, and he had begun to worry that soon she would stop altogether. This new request offered some hope.

'Well it's always difficult to learn a language straight from scratch Janet, and your French will go rusty without practice......'

'Oh I'm bored with French. I want to learn Italian. You speak it so well. I'll pay a bit extra if you like.'

'It's not a question of the money, Janet. I'll be glad to begin Italian with you. It's simply that as a valued client I thought you ought to know the difficulties.'

'Client? Surely more than that, Ted. We're friends.' She giggled at his sudden embarrassment. Quickly running to where he was standing she kissed him lightly, catching him off guard completely.

'So it's agreed then. We begin Italian next week. If not, then the week after. Yes?'

'Of course, of course.' He was still blushing and confused. He grabbed at something to say. 'But why Italian?'

'Because of the great country it is, the great nation it will become. Because of Signor Mussolini and the great work he is doing. Next summer I shall visit Italy. I shall meet him. Il Duce! There now, you see? I have made a start with my Italian already. Il Duce!'

The shells thudded all night. The mud was cold, numbing him, stiffening his uniform with a hard crust. The slightest movement dragged the wire through his skin, into his muscles. The pain was very great.

The Pacifist group always met in the church hall just next to the Three Tuns on the High Street. Amos Silverman was its main prop and central force and the meetings were always well attended. Punch did not always care for some of the politics but his commitment to pacifism was as deeply seated as ever.

How long the three young men had waited in the pub's doorway was hard to guess. They were getting edgy and cold by the time the meeting finished. They wanted this job over and done. They took Silverman first, a natural target.

'Jew bastard. Filthy Jew bastard.'

Two of them pounded and kicked the old man. The third turned to the horrified onlookers still grouped on the pavement.

'Who else loves Jews then? You?'

The street was dark and it had begun to rain. Punch didn't really see the man's face. He just felt a hand pull down his collar, forcing him into the gutters already streaming with mud.

The kicking began. He felt old wounds reopen, soaking his jacket and his shirt. Face down in the street he began to lose consciousness. Then he heard shouting and felt the blows stop. There were lots of voices and the weight of his attacker was pulled from him. He pushed upwards, twisting round. He saw lots of faces. One he recognised. A young man with large moustache and red cheeks. Punch groaned. An old score had been well settled.

They dumped him on a stretcher and scrambled back through the mud and wire. Not expecting him to survive the night and having many more there with much greater hopes, the doctors left him unattended until morning.

Punch knew about hospitals. When he began to recover he knew exactly where he was before his senses were fully restored. The smell, the white walls bouncing out footsteps and occasional voices, the stir and movement of a full ward.

The nurse beside him was speaking softly to a policeman who, when he saw Punch's eyes open, bent over him.

'Now then Mr. Roundtree. I'm sorry to see you in this bad way sir, very sorry indeed. I'm afraid I must bother you with a few questions though sir, if you feel up to it that is sir?'

Punch nodded.

'Thank you sir. I know you must be in great pain and I shall be as brief as possible. Then you can rest. The fact is sir, I have a name for you. I wonder if it means anything to you? The name is......'

'Atkinson.' He forced the word out. 'I saw him. Knew him as a boy. The man's name was Atkinson.'

The nurse looked down at her feet, the policeman coughed and shook his head slightly. Punch sensed embarrassment and concern.

'I beg your pardon Mr. Roundtree but it was Mr. Atkinson who dragged your assailant from you. Took a fair old swipe at him too.'

'Atkinson......at the meeting?'

'No sir, he was in the pub. He heard all the noise and rushed out. Tried to help poor Mr. Silverman, had a go at your chap and scared them all off.'

'I see.'

'The three of them hopped it then. Our lads got them, after

a bit of a chase.' Here he paused. 'No sir, the name I had in mind was Chatterton, Albert Chatterton. A Mosleyite of course. A really nasty bit of work.' He paused and lowered his voice. 'I'm sorry sir, I have to say it. You see, he claims you insulted his girlfriend. Claims an indelicacy occurred. You see if his attack can be proved spontaneous, hot-blooded if you like, as opposed to a calculated assault then it'll go a lot easier for him. I'm sorry Mr. Roundtree, I have to ask. Does the name Janet Byron mean anything? Do you know her at all sir?'

The gas was bitter. It burned his throat. If he twisted his head carefully he could see enemy lines heaped with sandbags, firmly dug in. Turning the other way, he saw his own lines, confused and empty. They put rifles in the hands of the dead and wounded, filled the trenches with bones. He pushed his face hard into the mud. The wire tightened around him as he rolled in its sharp embrace.

a personal essay

I wrote 'Out On The Wire' having been fascinated by an old family anecdote. It was about a teacher, badly hurt in World War 1, who believed that peace in Europe would be ensured if all the languages and cultures concerned were better understood by Europe's young people.

The specifics of the story I invented. That is the terrifying power of writing. You just make it up. Anything can happen to anybody, at any time, anywhere. This is very exciting for a writer. At the same time it is very frightening because you might make up the wrong things or you might miss bits out that are really important. I find that I need a core of truth that I can develop. I'm often the only one to know whether it's true or not and once I've found it I begin to explore as many possibilities as I can. When you work away at the process of making a story, the images and ideas run down your arm from your imagination and flood your pencil. To release that flood I need to begin with a fragment of fact. My own experiences and memories always come first.

This story is in many ways a very traditional one and contains deliberate echoes of writing produced in the later part of the last century and the early decades of this. However, alongside this method of telling a straightforward tale, I have used the idea of flashbacks. These are intensely visual and imagistic. They aim to drive home the story's meanings in a very direct way, as well as changing the rhythm and tone.

The problem a writer always faces is that a page of prose or poetry reveals its meaning as it is read, line by line. A painting on just the same size of paper conveys much more of its statement immediately. Of course you then have to return to it and dig deeper, but much of its impact is captured in a moment. As a writer I cannot rely on that at all. So in this story I constructed long strands of narrative which I broke up and contrasted with shorter, more sharply-focussed images. I hoped that this would create enough surprises and collisions to grip the readers' imagination and convince them of the story's meaning.

Another problem I faced was when the characters talked to each other. As I had chosen to write a story in which I attempted to give a sense of reality, I had to make the characters appear real as well. In a short story every word has to work hard; there can be no wastage, so the dialogue had to do several jobs. It had to reinforce meaning and carry forward the narrative. I could have chosen to have written in a very abstract way and not worried about 'reality' but these characters needed flesh and blood. They needed to almost walk in through the door, yet I had very little time in which to build them.

There are many stories to write; we are all full of them, crying out to be turned into fiction, but I did want to use this particular anecdote. I must have wanted to make some kind of statement with it.

It could be interpreted as saying that the naivity of Punch's Pacifism, his idealism, was easily broken up by the cruelty of Fascism and that such a simplistic idea could expect little else.

I was hoping to suggest something else though. I was hoping to say that any intricate, sensitive and enlightened view will have to struggle with a crude and violent opposition, as the countries facing Hitler were soon to discover, and that many battles will be lost before the war is won.

Punch lost his battle in the trenches but survived his war with life. He will leave the hospital at the end of the story as convinced as ever of the rightness of his views and as determined in his struggle.

In the end we all know that stories are a game, a pretence, an imagined set of people working through an imagined set of events that a writer has selected to make certain points. But it is that selectivity that allows fiction to be exciting and relevant, which allows it to float free from everyday circumstances and work in a heightened and self-aware way.

We are all able to write stories. What we need to learn and improve is the ability to select and fashion the imagined consequences of those stories so that we can entertain our readers and perhaps convey our perceptions to them as well. Like anybody else, it is a process I am still working through and expect I always shall be.

*a*n Incident In *The Ghobashi Household*

Zeinat woke to the strident call of the red cockerel from the rooftop above where she was sleeping. The Ghobashi house stood on the outskirts of the village and in front of it the fields stretched out to the river and the railway track.

The call of the red cockerel released answering calls from neighbouring rooftops. Then they were silenced by the voice of the *muezzin* from the lofty minaret among the mulberry trees calling: 'Prayer is better than sleep.'

She stretched out her arm to the pile of children sleeping alongside her and tucked the end of the old rag-woven *kilim* round their bodies, then shook her eldest daughter's shoulder.

'It's morning, another of the Lord's mornings. Get up, Ni'ma – today's market day.'

Ni'ma rolled onto her back and lazily stretched herself. Like someone alerted by the sudden slap of a gust of wind, Zeinat stared down at the body spread out before her. Ni'ma sat up and pulled her *galabia* over her thighs, rubbing at her sleep-heavy eyes in the rounded face with the prominent cheekbones.

'Are you going to be able to carry the grain to the market, daughter, or will it be too heavy for you?'

'Of course, mother. After all, who else is there to go?'

Zeinat rose to her feet and went out with sluggish steps to the courtyard, where she made her ablutions. Having finished the ritual prayer, she remained in the seated position as she counted off on her fingers her glorifications of Allah. Sensing that Ni'ma was standing behind her, she turned round to her:

'What are you standing there for? Why don't you go off and get the tea ready?'

Zeinat walked towards the corner where Ghobashi had stored the maize crop in sacks; he had left them as a provision for them after he had taken his air ticket from the office that had found him work in Libya and which would be bringing him back in a year's time.

'May the Lord keep you safe while you're away, Ghobashi,' she muttered.

Squatting in front of a sack, the grain measure between her thighs, she scooped up the grain with both hands till the measure was full, then poured it into a basket. Coughing, she waved away the dust that rose up to her face, then returned to her work.

The girl went to the large clay jar, removed the wooden covering and dipped the mug into it and sprinkled water on her face; she wetted the tips of her fingers and parted her plaits, then tied her handkerchief over her head. She turned to her mother:

'Isn't that enough, mother? What do we want the money for?'

Zeinat struck her knees with the palms of her hands and tossed her head back.

'Don't we have to pay off Hamdan's wage? – or was he cultivating the beans for us for nothing, just for the fun of hard work?'

Ni'ma turned away and brought the stove from the window shelf, arranging the dried corn-cobs in a pyramid and lighting them. She put it alongside her mother, then filled the teapot with water from the jar and thrust it into the embers. She squatted down and the two sat in silence. Suddenly Zeinat said:

'Since when has the buffalo been with young?'

'From after my father went away.'

'That's to say, right after the Great Feast, daughter?'

Ni'ma nodded her head in assent, then lowered it and began drawing lines in the dust.

'Why don't you go off and see how many eggs have been laid while the tea's getting ready.'

Zeinat gazed into the glow of the embers. She had a sense of peace as she stared into the dancing flames. Ghobashi had gone and left the whole load on her shoulders: the children, the two *kirats* of land and the buffalo. 'Take care of Ni'ma,' he had said the night before he left. 'The girl's body has ripened.' He had then spread out his palms and said: 'O Lord, for the sake of the Prophet's honour, let me bring back with me a marriage dress for her of pure silk.' She had said to him: 'May your words go straight from your lips to Heaven's gate, Ghobashi.' He wouldn't be returning before the following Great Feast. What would happen when he returned and found out the state of affairs? She put her head between the palms of her hands and leaned over the fire, blowing away the ashes. 'How strange,' she thought, 'are the girls of today! The cunning little thing was hanging out her towels at the time of her period every month just as though nothing had happened, and here she is in her fourth month and there's nothing showing.'

Ni'ma returned and untied the cloth from round the eggs, put two of them in the fire and the rest in a dish. She then brought two glasses and the tin of sugar and sat down next to her mother, who was still immersed in her thoughts.

'Didn't you try to find some way out?'

Ni'ma hunched her shoulders in a gesture of helplessness.

'Your father's been gone four months. Isn't there still time?'

'What's the use? If only the Lord were to spare you the trouble of me. Wouldn't it be for the best, mother, if my foot were to slip as I was filling the water jar from the canal and we'd be done with it?'

Zeinat struck herself on the breast and drew her daughter to her.

'Don't say such a wicked thing. Don't listen to such promptings of the Devil. Calm down and let's find some solution before your father returns.'

Zeinat poured out the tea. In silence she took quick sips at it, then put the glass in front of her and shelled the egg and bit into it. Ni'ma sat watching her, her fingers held round the hot glass. From outside came the raised voices of women discussing the prospects at the day's market, while men exchanged greetings as they made their way to the fields. Amidst the voices could be heard Hamdan's laughter as he led the buffalo to the two *kirats* of land surrounding the house.

'His account is with Allah,' muttered Zeinat. 'He's fine and doesn't have a worry in the world.'

Ni'ma got up and began winding round the end of her headcloth so as to form a pad on her head. Zeinat turned round and saw her preparing herself to go off to the market. She pulled her by her *galabia* and the young girl sat down again. At this moment they heard knocking at the door and the voice of their neighbour, Umm al-Khair, calling:

'Good health to you, folk. Isn't Ni'ma coming with me to market as usual, Auntie Zeinat? Or isn't she up yet?'

'Sister, she's just going off to stay with our relatives.'

'May Allah bring her back safely.'

Ni'ma looked at her mother enquiringly, while Zeinat placed her finger to her mouth. When the sound of Umm al-Khair's footsteps died away, Ni'ma whispered:

'What are you intending to do, mother? What relatives are you talking about?'

Zeinat got up and rummaged in her clothes box and took out a handkerchief tied round some money, also old clothes. She placed the handkerchief in Ni'ma's palm and closed her fingers over it.

'Take it – they're my life savings.'

Ni'ma remained silent as her mother went on:

'Get together your clothes and go straight away to the station and take a ticket to Cairo. Cairo's a big place, daughter, where you'll find protection and a way to make a living till Allah brings you safely to your time. Then bring it back with you at dead of night without anyone seeing you or hearing you.'

Zeinat raised the end of her *galabia* and put it between her teeth. Taking hold of the old clothes, she began winding them round her waist. Then she let fall the *galabia*. Ni'ma regarded her in astonishment:

'And what will we say to my father?'

'It's no time for talking. Before you go off to the station, help me up with the basket so that I can go to the market for people to see me like this. Isn't it better, when he returns, for your father to find himself with a legitimate son than an illegitimate grandson?'

The Ruum

The cruiser *Ilkor* had just gone into her interstellar overdrive beyond the orbit of Pluto when a worried officer reported to the Commander.

'Excellency,' he said uneasily, 'I regret to inform you that because of a technician's carelessness a Type H-9 Ruum has been left behind on the third planet, together with anything it may have collected.

The Commander's triangular eyes hooded momentarily, but when he spoke his voice was level.

'How was the ruum set?'

'For a maximum radius of 30 miles, and 160 pounds plus or minus 15.'

There was silence for several seconds, then the Commander said: 'We cannot reverse course now. In a few weeks we'll be returning, and can pick up the ruum then. I do not care to have one of those costly, self-energizing models charged against my ship. You will see,' he ordered coldly, 'that the individual responsible is severely punished.'

But at the end of its run, in the neighbourhood of Rigel, the cruiser met a flat, ring-shaped raider; and when the inevitable fire-fight was over, both ships, semi-molten, radioactive, and laden with dead, were starting a billion-year orbit around the star.

And on the earth, it was the age of reptiles.

When the two men had unloaded the last of the supplies, Jim Irwin watched his partner climb into the little seaplane. He waved at Walt.

'Don't forget to mail that letter to my wife,' Jim shouted.

'The minute I land,' Walt Leonard called back, starting to rev the engine. 'And you find us some uranium – a strike is just what Cele needs. A fortune for your son and her, hey?' His white teeth flashed in a grin. 'Don't rub noses with any grizzlies – shoot 'em, but don't scare 'em to death!'

Jim thumbed his nose as the seaplane speeded up, leaving a frothy wake. He felt a queer chill as the amphibian took off. For three weeks he would be isolated in this remote valley of the Canadian Rockies. If for any reason the plane failed to return to the icy blue lake, he would surely die. Even with enough food, no man could surmount the frozen peaks and make his way on foot over hundreds of miles of almost virgin wilderness. But, of course, Walt Leonard would return on schedule, and it was up to Jim whether or not they lost their stake. If there was any uranium in the valley, he had twenty-one days to find it. To work, then, and no gloomy forebodings.

Moving with the unhurried precision of an experienced woodsman, he built a lean-to in the shelter of a rocky over-hang. For this three weeks of summer, nothing more perma-nent was needed. Perspiring in the strong morning sun, he piled his supplies back under the ledge, well covered by a waterproof tarpaulin, and protected from the larger animal prowlers. All but the dynamite; that he cached, also carefully wrapped against moisture, two hundred yards away. Only a fool shares his quarters with a box of high explosives.

The first two weeks went by all too swiftly, without any encouraging finds. There was only one good possibility left, and just enough time to explore it. So early one morning, towards the end of his third week, Jim Irwin prepared for a last-ditch foray into the north-east part of the valley, a region he had not yet visited.

He took the Geiger counter, slipping on the earphones, reversed to keep the normal rattle from dulling his hearing, and reaching for the rifle, set out, telling himself it was now or never so far as this particular expedition was concerned. The bulky ·30–06 was a nuisance and he had no enthusiasm for its weight, but the huge grizzlies of Canada are not intruded upon with impunity, and take a lot of killing. He'd already had to dispose of two, a hateful chore, since the big bears were vanishing all too fast. And the rifle had proved a great comfort on several ticklish occasions when actual firing had been avoided. The ·22 pistol he left in its sheepskin holster in the lean-to.

He was whistling at the start, for the clear, frosty air, the bright sun on blue-white ice fields, and the heady smell of summer, all delighted his heart despite his bad luck as a prospector. He planned to go one day's journey to the new region, spend about thirty-six hours exploring it intensively, and be back in time to meet the plane at noon. Except for his emergency packet, he took no food or water. It would be easy enough to knock over a rabbit, and the streams were alive with firm-fleshed rainbow trout of the kind no longer common in the States.

All morning Jim walked, feeling an occasional surge of hope as the counter chattered. But its clatter always died down. The valley had nothing radioactive of value, only traces. Apparently they'd made a bad choice. His cheerfulness faded. They needed a strike badly, especially Walt. And his own wife, Cele, with a kid on the way. But there was still a chance. These last thirty-six hours – he'd snoop at night, if necessary – might be the pay-off. He reflected a little bitterly that it would help quite a bit if some of those birds he'd staked would make a strike and return his dough. Right this minute there were close to eight thousand bucks owing to him.

A wry smile touched his lips, and he abandoned unprofitable speculations for plans about lunch. The sun, as well as his stomach, said it was time. He had just decided to take out his line and fish a foaming brook, when he rounded a grassy knoll to come upon a sight that made him stiffen to a halt, his jaw dropping.

It was like like some enterprising giant's outdoor butcher shop: a great assortment of animal bodies, neatly lined up in a triple row that extended almost as far as the eye could see. And what animals! To be sure, those nearest him were ordinary deer, bear, cougars, and mountain sheep – one of each, apparently – but down the line were strange, uncouth, half-formed, hairy beasts; and beyond them a nightmare conglomeration of reptiles. One of the latter, at the extreme end of the remarkable display, he recognized at once. There had been a much larger specimen, fabricated about an incomplete skeleton, of course, in the museum at home.

No doubt about it – it was a small stegosaur, no bigger than a pony!

Fascinated, Jim walked down the line, glancing back over the immense array. Peering more closely at one scaly, dirty-yellow lizard, he saw an eyelid tremble. Then he realized the truth. The animals were not dead, but paralysed and miraculously preserved. Perspiration prickled his forehead. How long since stegosaurs had roamed this valley?

All at once he noticed another curious circumstance: the victims were roughly of a size. Nowhere, for example, was there a really large saurian. No tyrannosaurus. For that matter, no mammoth. Each specimen was about the size of a large sheep. He was pondering this odd fact, when the underbrush rustled a warning behind him.

Jim Irwin had once worked with mercury, and for a second it seemed to him that a half-filled leather sack of the liquid-metal had rolled into the clearing. For the quasi-spherical object moved with just a weighty, fluid motion. But it was not leather; and what appeared at first a disgusting wartiness, turned out on closer scrutiny to be more like the functional projections of some outlandish mechanism. Whatever the thing was, he had little time to study it, for after the spheroid had whipped out and retracted a number of metal rods with bulbous, lens-like structures at their tips, it rolled towards him at a speed of about five miles an hour. And from its purposeful advance, the man had no doubt that it meant to add him to the pathetic heap of living-dead specimens.

Uttering an incoherent exclamation, Jim sprang back a

number of paces, unslinging his rifle. The ruum that had been left behind was still some thirty yards off, approaching at that moderate but invariable velocity, an advance more terrifying in its regularity than the headlong charge of a mere brute beast.

Jim's hand flew to the bolt, and with practised deftness he slammed a cartridge into the chamber. He snuggled the battered stock against his cheek, and using the peep sight, aimed squarely at the leathery bulk – a perfect target in the bright afternoon sun. A grim little smile touched his lips as he squeezed the trigger. He knew what one of those 180-grain, metal-jacketed, boat-tail slugs could do at 2,700 feet per second. Probably at this close range it would keyhole and blow the foul thing into a mush, by God!

Wham! The familiar kick against his shoulder. E-e-e-e! The whining screech of a ricochet. He sucked in his breath. There could be no doubt whatever. At a mere twenty yards, a bullet from this hard-hitting rifle had glanced from the ruum's surface.

Frantically Jim worked the bolt. He blasted two more rounds, then realized the utter futility of such tactics.When the ruum was six feet away, he saw gleaming finger-hooks flick from warty knobs, and a hollow, sting-like probe, dripping greenish liquid, poised snakily between them. The man turned and fled.

Jim Irwin weighed exactly 149 pounds.

It was easy enough to pull ahead. The ruum seemed incapable of increasing its speed. But Jim had no illusions on that score. The steady five-mile-an-hour pace was something no organism on earth could maintain for more than a few hours. Before long, Jim guessed, the hunted animal had either turned on its implacable pursuer, or, in the case of more timid creatures, run itself to exhaustion in a circle out of sheer panic. Only the winged were safe. But for anything on the ground the result was inevitable: another specimen for the awesome array. And for whom the whole collection? Why? Why?

Coolly, as he ran, Jim began to shed all surplus weight. He glanced at the reddening sun, wondering about the coming night. He hesitated over the rifle; it had proved useless against the ruum, but his military training impelled him to keep the weapon to the last. Still, every pound raised the odds against him in the gruelling race he foresaw clearly. Logic told him that military reasoning did not apply to a contest like this; there would be no disgrace in abandoning a worthless rifle. And when weight became really vital, the ·30–06 would go. But meanwhile he slung it over one shoulder. The Geiger counter he placed as gently as possible on a flat rock, hardly breaking his stride.

One thing was damned certain. This would be no rabbit run, a blind panicky flight until exhausted, ending in squealing submission. This would be a fighting retreat, and he'd use every trick of survival he'd learned in his hazard-filled lifetime.

Taking deep, measured breaths, he loped along, watching with shrewd eyes for anything that might be used for his advantage in the weird contest. Luckily the valley was sparsely wooded; in brush or forest his straightway speed would be almost useless.

Suddenly he came upon a sight that made him pause. It was a point where a huge boulder overhung the trail, and Jim saw possibilities in the situation. He grinned as he remembered a Malay mantrap that had once saved his life. Springing to a hillock, he looked back over the grassy plain. The afternoon sun cast long shadows, but it was easy enough to spot the pursuing ruum, still oozing along on Jim's trail. He watched the thing with painful anxiety. Everything hinged upon this brief survey. He was right! Yes, although at most places the man's trail was neither the only route nor the best one, the ruum dogged the footsteps of his prey. The significance of that fact was immense, but Irwin had no more than twelve minutes to implement the knowledge.

Deliberatey dragging his feet, Irwin made it a clear trail directly under the boulder. After going past it for about ten yards, he walked backwards in his own prints until just short of the overhang, and then jumped up clear of the track to a point behind the balanced rock.

Whipping out his heavy-duty belt knife, he began to dig, scientifically, but with furious haste, about the base of the boulder. Every few moments, sweating with apprehension and effort, he rammed it with one shoulder. At last, it teetered a little. He had just jammed the knife back into his sheath, and was crouching there, panting, when the ruum rolled into sight over a small ridge on his back trail.

He watched the grey spheroid moving towards him and fought to quiet his sobbing breath. There was no telling what other senses it might bring into play, even though the ruum seemed to prefer just to follow in his prints. But it certainly had a whole battery of instruments at its disposal. He crouched low behind the rock, every nerve a charged wire.

But there was no change of technique by the ruum; seemingly intent on the footprints of its prey, the strange sphere rippled along, passing directly under the great boulder. As it did so, Irwin gave a savage yell, and thrusting his whole muscular weight against the balanced mass, toppled it squarely on the ruum. Five tons of stone fell from a height of twelve feet.

Jim scrambled down. He stood there, staring at the huge lump and shaking his head dazedly. 'Fixed that son of a bitch!' he said in a thick voice. He gave the boulder a kick. 'Hah! Walt and I might clear a buck or two yet from your little meat market. Maybe this expedition won't be a total loss. Enjoy yourself in hell where you came from!'

Then he leaped back, his eyes wild. The giant rock was shifting! Slowly its five-ton bulk was sliding off the trail, raising a ridge of soil as it grated along. Even as he stared, the boulder tilted, and a grey protuberance appeared under the nearest edge. With a choked cry, Jim Irwin broke into a lurching run.

He ran a full mile down the trail. Then finally, he stopped and looked back. He could just make out a dark dot moving away from the fallen rock. It progressed as slowly and as regularly and as inexorably as before, and in his direction. Jim sat down heavily, putting his head in his scratched, grimy hands.

But that despairing mood did not last. After all, he had gained a twenty-minute respite. Lying down, trying to relax as much as possible, he took the flat packet of emergency rations from his jacket, and eating quickly but without bolting, disposed of some pemmican, biscuit, and chocolate. A few sips of icy water from a streamlet, and he was almost ready to continue his fantastic struggle. But first he swallowed one of the three benzedrine pills he carried for physical crises. When the ruum was still an estimated ten minutes away, Jim Irwin trotted off, much of his wiry strength back, and fresh courage to counter bone-deep weariness.

After running for fifteen minutes, he came to a sheer face of rock about thirty feet high.The terrain on either side was barely passable, consisting of choked gullies, spiky brush, and knife-edge rocks. If Jim could make the top of this little cliff, the ruum surely would have to detour, a circumstance that might put it many minutes behind him.

He looked up at the sun. Huge and crimson, it was almost touching the horizon. He would have to move fast. Irwin was no rock climber but he did know the fundamentals. Using every crevice, roughness, and minute ledge, he fought his way up the cliff. Somehow – unconsciously – he used that flowing climb of a natural mountaineer, which takes each foothold very briefly as an unstressed pivot point in a series of rhythmic advances.

He had just reached the top when the ruum rolled up to the base of the cliff.

Jim knew very well that he ought to leave at once, taking advantage of the few precious remaining moments of daylight. Every second gained was of tremendous value; but curiosity and hope made him wait. He told himself that the instant his pursuer detoured he would get out of there all the faster. Besides, the thing might even give up and he could sleep right here.

Sleep! His body lusted for it.

But the ruum would not detour. It hesitated only a few seconds at the foot of the barrier. Then a number of knobs opened to extrude metallic wands. One of these, topped with lenses, waved in the air. Jim drew back too late – their uncanny gaze had found him as he lay atop the cliff, peering down. He cursed his idiocy.

Immediately all the wands retracted, and from a different knob a slender rod, blood-red in the setting sun, began to shoot straight up to the man. As he watched, frozen in place, its barbed tip gripped the cliff's edge almost under his nose.

Jim leaped to his feet. Already the rod was shortening as the ruum reabsorbed its shining length. And the leathery sphere was rising off the ground. Swearing loudly, Jim fixed his eyes on the tenacious hook, drawing back one heavy foot.

But experience restrained him. The mighty kick was never launched. He had seen too many rough-and-tumbles lost by an injudicious attempt at the boot. It wouldn't do at all to let any part of his body get within reach of the ruum's superb tools. Instead a length of dry branch, and inserting one end under the metal hook, began to pry.

There was a sputtering flash, white and lacy, and even through the dry wood he felt the potent surge of power that splintered the end. He dropped the smouldering stick with a gasp of pain, and wringing his numb fingers, backed off several steps, full of impotent rage. For a moment he paused, half inclined to run again, but then his upper lip drew back and, snarling, he unslung his rifle. By God! He knew he had been right to lug the damned thing all this way – even if it had beat a tattoo on his ribs. Now he had the ruum right where he wanted it!

Kneeling to steady his aim in the failing light Jim sighted at the hook and fired. There was a soggy thud as the ruum fell. Jim shouted. The heavy slug had done a lot more than he expected. Not only had it blasted the metal claw loose, but it had smashed a big gap in the cliff's edge. It would be pretty damned hard for the ruum to use that part of the rock again!

He looked down. Sure enough, the ruum was back at the bottom. Jim Irwin grinned. Every time the thing clamped a hook over the bluff, he'd blow that hook loose. There was plenty of ammunition in his pocket and, until the moon rose, bringing a good light for shooting with it, he'd stick the gun's muzzle inches away if necessary. Besides, the thing – whatever it might be – was obviously too intelligent to keep up a hopeless struggle. Sooner or later it would accept the detour. And then, maybe the night would help to hide his trail.

Then – he choked and, for a brief moment, tears came to his eyes. Down below, in the dimness, the squat, phlegmatic spheroid was extruding three hooked rods simultaneously in a fanlike spread. In a perfectly co-ordinated movement, the rods snagged the cliff's edge at intervals of about four feet.

Jim Irwin whipped the rifle to his shoulder. All right – this was going to be just like the rapid fire for record back at Benning. Only, at Benning, they didn't expect good shooting in the dark!

But the first shot was a bull's-eye, smacking the left-hand hook loose in a puff of rock dust. His second shot did almost as well, knocking the gritty stuff loose so the centre barb slipped off. But even as he whirled to level at number three, Jim saw it was hopeless.

The first hook was back in place. No matter how well he shot, at least one rod would always be in position, pulling the ruum to the top.

Jim hung the useless rifle muzzle down from a stunted tree and ran into the deepening dark. The toughening of his body, a process of years, was paying off now. So what? Where was he going? What could he do now? Was there anything that could stop the damned thing behind him?

Then he remembered the dynamite.

Gradually changing his course, the weary man cut back towards his camp by the lake. Overhead the stars brightened, pointing the way. Jim lost all sense of time. He must have eaten as he wobbled along, for he wasn't hungry. Maybe he could eat at the lean-to…no, there wouldn't be time… take a benzedrine pill. No, the pills were all gone and the moon was up and he could hear the ruum close behind. Close.

Quite often phosphorescent eyes peered at him from the underbrush and once, just at dawn, a grizzly whoofed with displeasure at his passage.

Sometimes during the night his wife, Cele, stood before him with outstretched arms. 'Go away!' he rasped. 'Go away! You can make it! It can't chase both of us.' So she turned and ran lightly alongside of him. But when Irwin panted across a tiny glade, Cele faded away into the moonlight and he realized she hadn't been there at all.

Shortly after sunrise Jim Irwin reached the lake. The ruum was close enough for him to hear the dull sounds of its passage. Jim staggered, his eyes closed. He hit himself feebly on the nose, his eyes jerked open and he saw the explosive. The sight of the greasy sticks of dynamite snapped Irwin wide awake.

He forced himself to calmness and carefully considered what to do. Fuse? No. It would be impossible to leave fused dynamite in the trail and time the detonation with the absolute precision he needed. Sweat poured down his body, his clothes were sodden with it. It was hard to think. The explosion *must* be set off from a distance and at the exact moment the ruum was passing over it. But Irwin dared not use a long fuse. The rate of burning was not constant enough. Couldn't calibrate it perfectly with the ruum's advance. Jim Irwin's body sagged all over, his chin sank toward his heaving chest. He jerked his head up, stepped back – and saw the ·22 pistol where he had left it in the lean-to.

His sunken eyes flashed.

Moving with frenetic haste, he took the half-filled case, piled all the remaining percussion caps among the loose sticks in a devil's mixture. Weaving out to the trail, he carefully placed box and contents directly on his earlier tracks some twenty yards from a rocky ledge. It was a risk – the stuff might go any time – but that didn't matter. He would far rather be blown to rags than end up living but paralysed in the ruum's outdoor butcher's stall.

The exhausted Irwin had barely hunched down behind the thin ledge of rock before his inexorable pursuer appeared over a slight rise five hundred yards away. Jim scrunched deeper into the hollow, then saw a vertical gap, a narrow crack between rocks. That was it, he thought vaguely. He could sight through the gap at the dynamite and still be shielded from the blast. If it was a shield ... when that half-case blew only twenty yards away....

He stretched out on his belly, watching the ruum roll forward. A hammer of exhaustion pounded his ballooning skull. Jesus! When had he slept last? This was the first time he had lain down in hours. Hours? Ha! It was days. His muscles stiffened, locked into throbbing, burning knots. Then he felt the morning sun on his back, soothing, warming, easing....No! If he let go, if he slept now, it was the ruum's macabre collection for Jim Irwin! Stiff fingers tightened around the pistol. He'd stay awake! If he lost – if the ruum survived the blast – there'd still be time to put a bullet through his brain.

He looked down at the sleek pistol, then out at the innocent-seeming booby trap. If he timed this right – and he would – the ruum wouldn't survive. No. He relaxed a little, yielding just a bit to the gently insistent sun. A bird whistled softly somewhere above him and a fish splashed in the lake.

Suddenly he was wrenched to full awareness. Damn! Of all times for a grizzly to come snooping about! With the whole of Irwin's camp ready for greedy looting, a fool bear had to come sniffing around the dynamite! The furred monster smelled carefully at the box, nosed around, rumbled deep displeasure at the alien scent of man. Irwin held his breath. Just a touch would blow a cap. A single cap meant....

The grizzly lifted his head from the box and growled hoarsely. The box was ignored, the offensive odour of man was forgotten. Its feral little eyes focused on a plodding spheroid that was now only forty yards away. Jim Irwin snickered. Until he had met the ruum the grizzly bear of the North American continent was the only thing in the world he had ever feared. And now – why the hell was he so calm about it? – the two terrors of his existence were meeting head on and he was laughing. He shook his head and the great side muscles in his neck hurt abominably. He looked down at his pistol, then out at the dynamite. *These* were the only real things in his world.

About six feet from the bear, the ruum paused. Still in the grip of that almost idiotic detachment, Jim Irwin found himself wondering again what it was, where it had come from. The grizzly arose on its haunches, the embodiment of utter ferocity. Terrible teeth flashed white against red lips. The business-like ruum started to roll past. The bear closed in, roaring. It cuffed at the ruum. A mighty paw, armed with black claws sharper and stronger than scythes, made that cuff. It would have disembowelled a rhinoceros. Irwin cringed as that sideswipe knocked dust from the leathery sphere. The ruum was hurled back several inches. It paused, recovered, and with the same dreadful casualness it rippled on, making a wider circle, ignoring the bear.

But the lord of the woods wasn't settling for any draw. Moving with that incredible agility which has terrified Indians,

Spanish, French and Anglo-Americans since the first encounter of any of them with his species, the grizzly whirled, side-stepped beautifully and hugged the ruum. The terrible, shaggy forearms tightened, the slavering jaws champed at the grey surface. Irwin half rose. 'Go it!' he croaked. Even as he cheered the clumsy emperor of the wild, Jim thought it was an insane tableau: the village idiot wrestling with a beach ball.

Then silver metal gleamed bright against grey. There was a flash, swift and deadly. The roar of the king abruptly became a whimper, a gurgle and then there was nearly a ton of terror wallowing in death – its throat slashed open. Jim Irwin saw the bloody blade retract into the grey spheroid, leaving a bright-red smear on the thing's dusty hide.

And the ruum rolled forward past the giant corpse, implacable, still intent on the man's spoor, his footprints, his pathway. Okay, baby, Jim giggled at the dead grizzly, this is for you, for Cele, for – lots of poor dumb animals like us – come to, you damned fool, he cursed at himself. And aimed at the dynamite. And very calmly, very carefully, Jim Irwin squeezed the trigger of his pistol.

Briefly, sound first. Then giant hands lifted his body from where he lay, then let go. He came down hard, face in a patch of nettles, but he was sick, he didn't care. He remembered that the birds were quiet. Then there was a fluid thump as something massive struck the grass a few yards away. Then there was quiet.

Irwin lifted his head...all men do in such a case. His body still ached. He lifted sore shoulders and saw... an enormous, smoking crater in the earth. He also saw, a dozen paces away, grey-white because it was covered now with powdered rock, the ruum.

It was under a tall, handsome pine tree. Even as Jim watched, wondering if the ringing in his ears would ever stop, the ruum rolled toward him.

Irwin fumbled for his pistol. It was gone. It had dropped somewhere, out of reach. He wanted to pray, then, but couldn't get properly started. Instead, he kept thinking, idiotically, 'My sister Ethel can't spell Nebuchadnezzar and never could. My sister Ethel—'

The ruum was a foot away now, and Jim closed his eyes. He felt cool, metallic fingers touch, grip, lift. His unresisting body was raised several inches, and juggled oddly. Shuddering, he waited for the terrible syringe with its green liquid, seeing the yellow, shrunken face of a lizard with one eyelid a-tremble.

Then, dispassionately, without either roughness or solicitude, the ruum put him back on the ground. When he opened his eyes, some seconds later, the sphere was rolling away. Watching it go, he sobbed dryly.

It seemed a matter of moments only, before he heard the seaplane's engine, and opened his eyes to see Walt Leonard bending over him.

Later, in the plane, five thousand feet above the valley, Walt grinned suddenly, slapped him on the back, and cried: 'Jim, I can get a whirlybird, a four-place job! Why, if we can snatch up just a few of those prehistoric lizards and things while the museum keeper's away, it's like you said – the scientists will pay us plenty.'

Jim's hollow eyes lit up. 'That's the idea,' he agreed. Then, bitterly: 'I might just as well have stayed in bed. Evidently the damned thing didn't want me at all. Maybe it wanted to know what I paid for these pants! Barely touched me, then let go. And how I ran!'

'Yeah,' Walt said. 'That was damned queer. And after that marathon. I admire your guts, boy.' He glanced sideways at Jim Irwin's haggard face. 'That night's run cost you plenty. I figure you lost over ten pounds.'

DOROTHY HAYNES

*T*he Cure

The women came early, calling and crowding at the door. 'Are you ready, Missis? We thought we'd go with you for the company, like. Just one or two of us....'

'You might want some help with the boy.'

She had not bargained for that. All night she had lain awake and worried, and now she had made up her mind. She would do as the neighbours said; but if David was to go, he must go with her alone, so that he could change his mind and run back if he wanted to. After all, he might be twelve years old, but he was little more than a baby.

She told them, but they would not listen. 'You're too soft with him, Mrs Weir. I wouldn't put up with his capers.'

'It's time he started acting like a man. With his father gone, you could do with a man in the house.'

His lips were white, but she kept her temper, seeing their food on the table, and so many other things, the very coat the boy was wearing. 'I told you I'd bring him. You can come if you want to; but I'll need time. It's not a thing you can do in a minute.'

They withdrew, not very willingly, and she stood crumpling

her apron, looking down at her son. The clock whirred, but did not strike, and the lid of the kettle lifted on a slow puff of steam. 'Come on, David,' she said, trying to force a sprightliness into her voice. 'Wash your face, now. I've warmed the water for you.'

The boy did not answer. He hardly ever answered, and sometimes she wondered if he heard properly. Unless, of course, it was too much bother to him to speak. Everything was a bother to him nowadays.

'Do you hear me, son? You can't go up dirty.'

The child began to blubber, his face turned to the fire. 'I don't want to go,' he mumbled. 'I don't *want* to!'

A finger tapped at the window, and a face peered through the pane, and suddenly, her anger at the neighbours was transferred to her son, so that, for the moment, the fear of failure was less than the fear of his being a coward. She went over to the fire and shook the snivelling boy by the shoulder. 'Get up now, David. Wash your face and get outside. Do you think your father made this fuss when *he* went?'

It was cruel, but the snivelling stopped. Wiping his eyes, David got up and laved his eyes at the basin. His legs trembled, thin as sticks, but he said nothing as his mother brushed the hair out of his eyes and straightened his clothes. 'Now,' she said, 'it's for you own good, son. Don't look, don't think. Just walk straight on, and keep your eyes shut at the end...'

Holding his hand, her own hand trembling, she led him outside, and his weak eyes screwed against the sun. The clouds were incredibly white, puffed up and sailing, the trees and grass too green to be true. He had not been out for so long... the brightness puckered her own forehead, so that she looked at the ground; and then she forced herself to face the neighbours.

They stared at her, impatient, their faces half hidden in their great hoods, and she could see that they were itching to get away up the hill. She did not want to see them gabbing and whispering in front of her. Her lips quivering, she held her son's hand tighter, and went to the head of the procession.

They went slowly, because the road was bad, full of spring puddles and ruts and potholes. There were great splashes of dung where cattle had passed, and all the gutters were swimming. The houses leaned over the street, one side in sun, the other in shadow, and everywhere windows opened, and heads poked out to ask questions. 'Davie Weir,' the women who were following told them. 'Going to be *touched*. Him whose father was hanged,' and the word was passed back eagerly, impatiently, to the old folk by the fire. 'Dick Weir's wife. Taking her son to the gallows. Up to the *gallows!*'

'Oh!' They had heard of it, this dreadful thing, the old superstition that the touch of a hanged corpse could heal, but few of them had seen it carried out. There weren't so many hangings nowadays. There had been no excitement in the town since Dick Weir had been hoisted a month ago, and there were some people who said that the law had been too hard on him. Weir had always been a sober, steady man, but his son was a weakling, never without coughs or fevers or aches in his bones, and the only way for a poor man to get medicine and dainties was by stealing.

Well, now that he was dead, it looked as if he might be more use to the boy than when he was alive. It was worth going to find out. The weavers came from their narrow houses, fluff in their hair, their looms silent. The baker left his shop, and a smell of new bread came with him, warm and delicious. He stuck his floury hands in his apron and ambled after the crowd, and the blacksmith left his forge to the apprentice and the horses stamping and jingling in the gloom. 'Going to be *touched*,' they mouthed, and nodded to each other. 'Dick Weir's son,' and they shook their heads with the pity of it; but there was a brightness and stir about the morning, just as there had been a month ago, and more of the people followed on, Old Andra, the bellringer, the two idiots who were propped all day against the church railings, and a squatter of children whose mothers were glad to be rid of them for a while.

The woman walked on, leading her son, seeing and acknowledging no-one. She had not been out since the hanging, and it was like the first walk after illness, lightheaded and unreal. She could not fix her mind on what would happen at the top of the hill; and maybe Dick had been the same. It should have been a comfort to her; but surely he must have realised, as the chains were put on him, and he faced away over the wide view...He had always been an outdoor man. He must have screamed and fought, if he were human. She herself, sitting with the boy, had stuffed her hands into her mouth till she choked. Outside, the noise had increased, and then quietened again, except for one awful sound, like a groan or a sigh, that she heard, and yet did not hear; then the people had come back to the streets again, in twos and threes, but they did not tell her what it had been like. 'He carried himself well,' was all they said.

They had been more than good to her. She had looked for work, cleaning or washing at the big houses, but nobody would employ a woman whose husband had been hanged. It was the neighbours who kept her going with small gifts, oil for the lamp, loaves and logs, and their company in case she felt lonely.

Sometimes she almost longed for loneliness. They were kind, but they never left her, talking, talking from dawn till dark. They sat about the kitchen, loath to forget about the hanging and let the excitement die. She did not want to speak about her husband. What she wanted was quiet to remember him – or to forget. They asked about David, and tried to rally him, and laugh him out of his turns, and she could not explain that David did not like to be teased. Everything was out of order. There was spilt milk on the table, and the fire smouldered bitterly; but without the neighbours there would have been no milk and no fire.

And then, out of kindness, they made their suggestion, a word, a nudge, a hint behind the hands.

'They say it's a great cure, Missis. Rachael, the orphan, they took her....'

'You owe it to your son, Missis. What's a wee unpleasantness? He's not too far gone....'

'No!' she screamed at them. 'I couldn't! It's not right....'

'It's his own father,' they argued. 'If you thought anything of the boy...'

She was angry at that, but they kept their patience, talk, talk, talk, till at last, out of weariness and dutiful gratitude, she gave in.

Up past the school, where the houses began to thin out, the path mounted the hill. Lambs leaped, wobbly-legged, and the turf smelled sweet. They climbed like pilgrims, stopping sometimes because the boy was tired, and soon the ones behind began to press forward to see what was happening. They looked ahead, pointing to the top of the hill, but Mrs Weir and her son never looked up. She kept her head down, and led the boy by the arm, like a blind man.

The ground was levelling now, and a wind blew against their faces. The woman felt rather than saw what was about her; behind, the babble of voices, and in front, nothing but a faint swish, like cloth rubbing on wood, and a sickly smell....

The boy looked sideways at her, for guidance. His face was sick, green-looking, but she could not help him. She could not lift her hand to cover her eyes, although what was above seemed to be drawing her. She stood there, as if in prayer, and there was nothing she could do. Nothing.

Suddenly, one of the women pushed forward, grabbed the boy by the waist, and half lifted him. 'Go on, son. Up. Let him touch you.'

Something creaked, and chains clinked a little. Other hands lifted him up from behind, thrusting roughly, hurting him. 'That's it. His hand....'

He was light in their arms, for all his struggles. His eyes were tight shut, but his fists threshed pettishly, landing weak blows on arms and faces. Higher they pushed him, and there was something on his shoulder, cold, listless, something that slid off again uncaringly. The boy began to scream, shrilly, thinly, and at the sound his mother looked up, in spite of herself.

She made no sound, but her breath gagged back in her mouth, and her face was grey. This limp thing, bumping about like a sack, this was not her husband. If it had been recognisable, it would have broken her heart. Now, she felt only fear of it, the thin hair fluttering, the faint whiff of decay as it swung. Even the clamorous women were retreating, their handkerchiefs spread to their faces. The body turned again, grinning, and suddenly she felt herself swinging round with it, round and round and down in a cold dampness and roaring....

And then, her son was beside her, no longer screaming. His thin arms circled her, his slight body leaned in to support her. There were tears on his cheeks, and his mouth puckered childishly with crying, but there was the first hint of maturity in his face. 'Get away!' he shouted to the crowds pressing in to stare at him. 'Get away from her. Can't you leave us alone?'

'Davie!' His mother shivered, and pulled at his sleeve to quieten him. 'Mind yourself now, Davie. They wanted to help –'

'Look at them,' he said.

Her hands at her mouth, her mouth nibbling, she looked, and the hooded women stared back at her, callous, curious, licking their lips over the drama. For a moment, it seemed to her that the judge and the hangman were innocent, and that these were the real people who had strung her husband on the gibbet.

But now it no longer mattered. She stood in a daze, her hands still at her mouth, and her son seemed to tower above her, older, wiser, with infinite power to protect. As he pushed forward, they fell away on each side of him, the weavers, the blacksmith, and the mob who had followed for the fun of it. He passed through them without a glance. They stood for all the things he had learned and spurned at the foot of the gallows – the poverty that forced a man to steal, the cruelty of those who hanged him; and the ignorance of those who, even now, were rejoicing that the touch of a hanged corpse could really heal.

HAZEL D. CAMPBELL

*S*ee Me In Me
Benz And T'ing

Like The Lady Who Lived
On That Isle Remote

The Lady of the house sucked her teeth angrily as she put down the telephone.

'Carl knows I can't stand driving down to his factory,' she complained loudly.

'Why doesn't he just send the driver for the car!' she gestured in annoyance. 'In a hurry, my foot!'

The maid dusting the furniture nearby didn't comment as she knew her place better than that. In any case she wasn't being directly addressed.

'Don't forget the upstairs sitting room,' the Lady ordered, suddenly turning her annoyance on the maid. 'Yesterday I ran my finger over the TV up there. Absolutely filthy! Don't know why it's so difficult to get you people to do an honest day's work.'

Carl had absolutely ruined her day, the Lady pouted. She would be late for the session with the girls and miss all the nice gossip. Furthermore Carl knew that she hated driving through the section of the city where he worked. So much violence, and all those people glaring at her in hostility as if she were personally responsible for the squalor in which they lived. Like wild animals some of them with their uncombed heads and crazy talk. Watching her as if any minute they

115

would attack. No wonder the papers were always full of horrible stories about them. Now she wouldn't even have time to do
her nails and she had so wanted to show off the new shade
Sylvia had brought back from Miami for her. Damn that Carl!

Quarrelling with the maid, the gardener and the two Alsa-
tians blocking her path to the car, she gathered her purse and
her keys and got into the sleek black Status Symbol which had
been resting in the double carport.

The 4.5 litre, V8 engine sprang alive and settled into a
smooth purr before she eased into reverse, turned it around
and put it into drive to make the long trip from home on the
hilltop to workplace by the seashore. It gathered speed as she
rolled down the hill, and, as always, she felt a tiny moment of
panic at the strength of the horsepower growling softly under
the bonnet, controlled only by the swift movement of foot
from accelerator to brake as necessary. Carl had promised her
this car if ever he was able to buy a newer one, but since 1972,
no new models had been allowed into the island so she had to
be content with the Mazda, which didn't satisfy her vanity half
as much as the Status Symbol did.

Annoyance returned sharply as she imagined how the girls
would have exclaimed when she drove up in the Benz.

'Eh! Eh! How you manage get Carl to part with his car?' they
would tease. And she would explain that the Mazda was in
the garage so she had to borrow the Benz, pretending with
them that it was these great big problems which made life so
difficult. Then they would settle down to a nice chat about the
Number of Things they were having to do without! And Who
had just gone, or Who had decided to! And pass a pleasant
hour or so laughing at the kinds of things some people were
packing into trailers. And had they heard that Jonesie was
working in a shoe store in Miami as a sales clerk! No! God forbid! And *my dearing*, and *oh dearing* each other, they would
with large eyes contemplate life in the 70s in Jamaica, each
realizing, but not saying that they did not know how to come
to grips with it.

As the Lady skirted the Sealand trailer parked at the foot of
the hill, she remembered that she wanted to renew her cam-
paign to get Carl to migrate. After all he could even pack the

factory machinery in the trailer, she thought, and they could relocate in Florida. Lots of other people were doing it. Things were really getting impossible. Imagine, not even tampons in the shops. Good thing she knew many people who were still commuting between America and Jamaica, so she could get a ready supply of the things she absolutely couldn't do without.

As she passed through Half-Way-Tree, the Lady collected her wandering thoughts. She would need all her concentration to get safely through the congested parts of the city she would soon be entering. Just last week a friend of theirs had been pulled from his car and savagely beaten because he had scraped somebody's motorcycle with the car.

She made sure all the doors were locked, touched the power button for the windows and turned on the air conditioning. She was always grateful for the ability to lock up herself in the car. Lock out the stenches of gutters and overcrowded human flesh. Lock out the sounds of human distress. From the cool, slight dimness of the red interior of the Status Symbol, even the sight of distress took on a sort of unreal appearance, so she could pass through uncontaminated.

A little past Half-Way-Tree, she hesitated a moment before deciding to turn down Maxfield Avenue. She hated cutting across Spanish Town Road, but this way was shorter, and Carl had said to hurry. That was why he hadn't sent somebody for the car. The double journey would take too long. She had wasted enough time already, so she would have to hurry. She was afraid of Carl's bad temper. He would lash out at her even in front of the factory staff if he was sufficiently annoyed. She was sure it wasn't all that important for him to get the car. Probably some luncheon or other for which he needed the Status Symbol to impress somebody. He wouldn't dream of driving one of the small company cars. Not him. No matter how it inconvenienced her.

By the time she reached the first set of lights, the traffic had already begun to crawl. Not much use her ability to move from 0 to 60 miles per hour in ten seconds flat, here. Not much use all that horse power impatiently ticking under her restraining foot. Thank God for the air conditioning, she thought again.

As she waited for the green light, the billboard on top of the shop at the corner caught her eye. 'LIFE IS A MUTUAL AFFAIR' it read. Somebody ought to tell Carl that. Instead of dragging her through this horrid part of town he should be protecting her. Any moment now a bullet could shatter the glass and kill her.

She spent a moment indulging her overactive imagination, seeing her blood-splattered breast and she leaning back as still as she had seen a body in some film or other. The impatient horn behind her made her suddenly realize that the lights had changed.

She moved off quickly, smiling at her melodramatic thoughts. Actually she wasn't feeling too afraid. After all, didn't Carl do this trip everyday? And if there were problems outside, she couldn't hear.

That group of people milling around outside that shop, for instance, she couldn't see what was creating the excitement and since she couldn't hear either, what did it matter? They were like puppets in a silent movie. In fact she could not decide what they were doing. Was it a dead man they were looking at?

Christ! Her imagination! She really must do something about it, she thought. Wonder if she was getting off. Lots of people getting crazy these days, because of all the stress and strain, she'd heard. They were probably just fassing in somebody's business as usual, idle bitches, that they were. Look at those on that other piazza. Winding up themselves and gyrating to some beat loud enough to penetrate her castle of silence. That's all they were good for. And those others milling around the betting shop, race forms in hand. How could the country progress with so many idlers never wanting to do any work? And even those who said they worked couldn't do a thing. Her annoyance deepened as she thought how she couldn't get Miriam to clean the bathrooms properly. No amount of telling did the trick. No matter how often she told her what to do. No matter what amount of cleaning things she bought.

The traffic began to crawl again as she neared Spanish Town Road. Just at the part she would have liked to pass over quickly. Now she had plenty of time to look out through her smoky glass at unreality.

Another billboard. Advertising Panther. Good-looking youth, she thought. Not like the dirty bums cotching up the walls, the street posts, and any fence strong enough to bear their weight. The Panther boy looked like somebody who would care about life and not spawn too many children. But what did he have to do with these dirty creatures passing as men around the place? Giving all those worthless women thousands of children by the minute. Silly ad, she thought. Silly place to put it.

Ah! There was her favourite on the other side. Beautiful clouds and a jet taking off into the sunset – FASTEST WAY TO CANADA – She liked to think about that. Escape from the closing-in feeling of Jamaica. It was only a matter of time, her friends were saying, before all of Kingston and St Andrew looked like these dumps around her. Zinc fences hiding poverty and nastiness, hate and crime. Smells she could only imagine now. People living, no, not living, existing on top of each other. God forbid that she should ever live like that. That she should even live close to this. Bad enough to have to drive through.

Suddenly she realized that none of the cars was moving, neither up nor down, and that there was an unusual amount of people on the streets even for this crowded area.

What could be the matter? she thought in alarm.

Then she noticed the driver in front of her turning up his car windows in haste, seconds before she saw the first part of the crowd running between the cars. Running in her direction.

Oh God! She prayed softly. Had it finally happened? Were they going to get her? Stories she had heard about riots and those who got caught in them raced through her thoughts.

But even in her panic she still felt fairly safe. Wasn't she protected in her air-conditioned car? People were swarming around like the cartoon figures on Spider Man, the TV show her children were always watching. And she was looking on at the action, as if she were in a drive-in movie, with a larger-than-life screen surrounding her. But even as she watched, the sounds of their distress began to filter into her castle.

She wondered what was happening, but dared not open

her window to find out. To do that would be to let in reality which would force her to think and act. Better to stay locked up in the car and hope that whatever it was would allow her to get moving soon.

In the distance she saw something like a wisp of smoke and thought perhaps it might be fire. But why would the people be running away from it? And why did they look so frightened?

And even as she noticed their fright it turned to anger right before her eyes. One minute they were running away from something, wave after wave of them. The next, like a freeze in a movie, a pause, long enough to allow anger to replace fright. A turn around. And then hell breaking loose.

She could tell by the shape of their mouths that they were angry. By their swoops for weapons that they were angry.

From nowhere, it seemed, sticks, stones and bottles appeared and began to fly around.

The car, she panicked. They would scratch the car, and what would Carl say? That the damn ducoman wouldn't match the shade and he would have to do over the whole car – if there was any duco available? Funny how Carl's anger about a scratched car was more real to her than the anger of the mass of people milling around about her, getting hurt, hurting and going mad with anger for what reason she didn't even know.

The traffic going in the opposite direction had somehow managed to move on, and those behind her were frantically trying to turn around to escape the mob.

The Lady, tense and nervous, put the car into reverse and put her finger on the horn hoping that they would clear the way for her to turn around. But all she did was to bring down their wrath on her. The reality of their anger began to reach her when she felt the human earthquake rocking the car. A human earthquake fed by anger. Anger now turned against the Status Symbol in their midst. The out-of-place Symbol.

The driver before her had abandoned his car. The doors were wide open with people like ants tearing off the wings of an injured beetle. Oh! God! There was one of the mad men trying to open her door to pull her out. To destroy her. She didn't need to hear them yelling, 'Mash it up! Mash it up!' She shut her eyes in pain as the shattering sound reached her and the stone which had smashed the windscreen settled on the seat beside her, letting in reality. The reality of angry sounds, angry smells, demented faces and nightmare hands grabbing her.

She didn't hear herself screaming as they dragged her from the car, roughly discarding her to fight as best she could. They weren't interested in her. Only in the Symbol. The Symbol must be destroyed. The insulting Symbol, black as their bodies, inside red as their blood.

Mash it up! Not just a scratch. Damage it beyond repair. Rip out its red heart. Turn it over. And just to make sure, set it on fire. Destroy it forever.

The Lady stood in the crowd, assaulted by forgotten humanity, and she still didn't feel their reality. She was remembering the day her husband had brought the car home. The first year the factory had made a profit he had ordered this car to celebrate. *'This is the symbol, baby,'* he'd said. *'The symbol that we've arrived.'* That was why, between them, they jokingly referred to it as the Status Symbol.

Her feelings now were tied up with the Symbol's destruction. Her blood scattered in the streets. Her flesh being seared by the fire. And the sudden roar of the flames as the Symbol caught fire pulled a scream of animal rage from the very bowels of her.

But the roar of the sacrifice quieted the mob's anger. As quickly as they had come they began to melt away.

The Lady didn't notice. The Lady didn't hear herself bawling. Neither did she feel the gentle hands of the two old women steering her away from the scene of her destruction.

'Thank God is only the car!' they whispered, as they hurried her away from the street, down a lane and into a yard. They took her behind one of the zinc fences, into the safety of their humanity. 'Sometimes the people them not so fortunate,' they murmured as they bathed her cuts and bruises and gave her some sweet sugar and water to drink. 'You is lucky is only this happen to you.'

And they didn't ask her name. For them it wasn't important who she was. She needed help and they gave what they could without question, fear or favour.

SUE WILSEA

Double Vision

'Runt, runt!' the kids would jeer as Jacko darted, skipped and weaved through the straggling groups making their way up the school drive. I don't know if they knew what 'runt' meant; perhaps they just liked the sound of the woody word that was so much like a rude one. At any rate, they were right about his size – he was small, very small, and he had a habit of thrusting one shoulder and then the other forward and up as if trying to jolt himself into growth. He was also dirty, but not with the kind of dirt that makes so many little boys endearing; this was engrained, etched into his palms, his neck, his knees. The smell that this kind of encrusted grime exuded was stale but rather sweet.

Jacko was cross-eyed and short-sighted and it was difficult to believe that the flimsy pair of pink national health spectacles, taped over the bridge where they were regularly broken in fights, could remedy either of these defects. He would bark rather than talk at you, asking questions, continually demanding, and the questions would pin you, hold you and Jacko would have what he craved more than anything – your attention. Like a scruffy performing monkey, Jacko would do anything for attention. He was rumoured to have eaten a bowl of dogfood for a bet, although it was quite possible that hunger played a part too.

I started work just after Christmas. The class Jacko was in consisted of twenty boys and four girls, the latter for the most part being the butt of sexual innuendo from the boys. Most of them were leaving at Easter and, even worse than being overtly aggressive and disruptive, they were cynically resigned to what lay ahead. Occasionally they turned to Jacko for entertainment....

'Go on, Jacko, you tell 'er.'

'He's a bloody nutter, Jacko is.'

But for the most part the class and I enjoyed a mutual tolerance.

Jacko was a different matter. He was adept at spotting weakness, prodding it, rubbing at it until it erupted. For much of the time, I hated him; at times I could feel the fury starting upwards from the pit of my stomach and I knew I needed to vent this violence. I'd felt the same way towards my own child at times, wanting to hurt, to pull, to punish. Normally, the one part of myself that remained sane and rational ensured the release was exacted on a chair, a door or something similar. But this one day was to be different.

If Jacko had one undisputed talent it was for mimicry. There had been an attempt in the past by a young, hopelessly enthusiastic teacher, naively sure that all social barriers could be broken down, to channel this ability into the school drama group but, not unexpectedly, it failed. The gentle cultured atmosphere of the latter had been alien to Jacko and he to it. Their cruelty was subtle – no shouts of 'runt' here – middle class courtesy was as engrained in them as Jacko's dirt. However, it was the slight wrinkling of the nose, barely noticeable, as he passed or the quick glance downwards at his battered gym-shoes that gave them away; he was not one of them and the free-thinking, free-wheeling Drama Group (Meets Mondays 3:45 Room 7 – Come Along and Do Your Own Thing) brought their shutters down firmly. He, for his part, mimicked them in an accurate and deadly way, capturing their self-conscious posturing exactly.

'Poufs' was his unequivocal opinion of them.

On this particular occasion, it was as if Jacko had intuitively sensed that my spirits were ragged. Earlier that morning, Chris, my son, and I had clawed and torn at each other's feelings in the way that only people who are close to each other do. I don't remember what had actually sparked it off – perhaps an untidy room or a missing sock or a stain on the carpet – and anyway, it doesn't matter; both of us would seize on that kind of domestic niggle as fuel for the resentment and anger that were never far from the surface. It was tempting, sometimes useful, to attribute these scenes to the pressures of being a one-parent family but I never quite convinced myself. Jacko, not surprisingly, came from a one-parent family too but that no more explained his neglect than did his address or his height or his name. In fact, there were some physical similarities between Jacko and Chris. Naturally, Chris was clean and well cared for, nothing wrong with his eyesight either, but they were about the same size despite Chris being the younger. There was something about the look they both fixed one with, the look that demanded, instilled guilt and inadequacy, that was belligerent and at the same time supplicatory.

'What on earth do you mean?' Chris' father had exploded impatiently when, several months earlier, I had attempted to explain this to him. As he spoke, he was packing things into the big brown battered case which had accompanied us on all the family holidays. Another business trip. More time when Chris and I would be caged together. 'You're always going on about looks and feelings and atmospheres. Always analysing and probing and questioning. Why can't you just take life as it comes and enjoy it?'

'Like you do, I suppose,' I'd retorted bitterly. 'Look, I'm simply trying to make you see how explosive it is here. Chris puts all the pressure on me and it should be on you as well.'

'I can't help being away a lot of the time. What do you expect me to do? Give up my job and we'll all live off your income?'

'No, of course not, but sometimes I'm afraid that...'

'It's eight o'clock and I've got to go.' He snapped the case to and swung it off the bed. 'Look, Chris is fit and happy. He's got friends, he's doing well at school and he's got his football. O.K., so you have rows but I'm sure that's the same with all teenagers. I must go. I'll ring you tonight.'

It was very shortly after this that he had left us for good. Then I was ill for a while and the tension had eased between Chris and me. But now, this morning, we had reached the brink once more.

'God, call yourself a mother!' He was standing at the front door, sports bag over his shoulder, playing with the latch but unwilling to go.

'Don't speak to me like that! Who do you think you are? Show some respect.'

'Respect is earned, not yours by right.'

'Very clever, aren't you?'

'You're proud of my ability when it suits you.'

'I'm not proud of you right now, Chris.'

'Snap.' He fixed me with that clear challenging look and I had to turn away.

So that when I walked into that classroom that morning it was a few moments before I fully realised what was going on. I entered the room from the back, by way of a large store cupboard that linked my room with another – not my usual way and obviously not expected. Jacko was entertaining the rest of the class, who were sitting around on desk-tops and leaning against the windows, by doing a superb and deadly impersonation of me. All my idiosyncrasies were laid bare – the twiddling with an earring, the repeated use of 'Right then folks' as a prelude to anything I had to say, my slightly pigeon-toed walk, everything. It was like suddenly catching sight of oneself in a large mirror in a shop, for a split second not knowing who it is, and than having a swamping realisation of the truth. That was not all. To the obvious delight of the class, Jacko was also repeating an anecdote I had told them the previous week. We had been doing some work on the topic of 'The Family' and I had recounted some insignificant but amusing tale of Chris as a little boy. It had been a good lesson, most of them had swapped stories and there had been laughter, though Jacko had not said anything.

Now, in a couple of steps I was at Jacko's shoulder while he, unaware, was still in mid-performance. All that I could grasp was that a grotesque parody of myself was being enacted for cheap entertainment. I suppose my vanity was dented but there was anger too at how this little boy could hurt me. His use of my story was like a violation of my son somehow, as if Jacko was the dark, the negative side of my son. Perhaps a psychologist would explain my actions as revenge against the whole of the male sex, as retribution for the wrongs done to me by little boys who had become older. Be that as it may, I certainly did not think what I did. I simply hit him hard on the side of his face and as he yelped and ducked, I hit again and then again. When I stopped I found I was panting and my hand was stinging. He had darted behind a desk and squinted up at me. Our eyes met and held and whether it was Chris' face or Jacko's I don't know because I was crying. It was over very quickly; the rest of the class had sheepishly found their way to their places and were half-heartedly getting out books, papers and folders. As for Jacko, he just stood there, one little shoulder thrust forward and a grubby hand rubbing at the side of his head. His expression was difficult to make out.

'Christ, you don't 'alf pack a punch, miss, there's a bloody lump coming up on me 'ead. I could sprag on yer and you'd get the push. Yer not meant to clout us anymore. And me specs have bust again...'

Strangely, that was the worst moment of all for his tone made clear what he felt and what his expression had been. Although complaining because it was expected of him, he actually admired and even respected me because I had behaved the same way as all the other adults in his life had done. He now understood me and there was no way he was going to 'sprag' on me to the authorities. So much for the patient, caring and peace-loving teacher and mother. I turned and left the room, told the office I had a severe migraine, and went home.

When Chris arrived back, about five-thirty, I was sitting in the front room in the half-light, the curtains not drawn and the fire not yet lit.

'What's up, Mum? Are you alright?' He flung his bag and his jacket onto the table, looking worried and a little embarrassed;

anything 'female' made him ill at ease, although he had been very supportive all the time I had been unwell the previous year.

'Chris, do you think I'm a good mother?' How inadequate I sounded even to myself.

He was immediately and understandably irritated 'What sort of a question is that? How do I know what a good mother is? I dunno …. Yeh, I suppose you are …. of course you are …' He softened. 'Sorry about this morning, I know I get you riled and you're not meant to get upset. What's the matter? Are you poorly?'

'Oh, it's nothing really. I came back from school early. Migraine.'

'Right, I'll get you one of your tablets, shall I?' Chris sounded relieved, he liked things to be clear, hated ambiguity.

'Yes, thanks. They're on the kitchen table – and get me a glass of water.'

The room was nearly dark now; it was soothing and I closed my eyes and let the evening sounds wash over me: papers thudding through letter boxes, the click-clack of heels on the pavement, strains of the news at 5.45. My thoughts were half-formed and hazy and I drifted….

Just after I'd started work I'd set Jacko's class a piece of writing on their Christmas holidays. The banality of the task set was matched by most of the efforts which had merely consisted of lists of expensive gifts – computers, digital watches, personal stereos and the like. Jacko had gripped a stub of pencil in his fist and had laboriously produced a few closely-written lines dug into the paper. I'd later managed, with his help, to decipher the fact that he'd received a selection box of sweets from his Mum.

'It wasn't one of them small 'uns though, Miss. It was huge and it had three Mars bars an' a Twix an' Smarties. An' on the back it had one of them games but me Mum threw the box out by mistake.'

Poor kid. Deprived kid. Did his mother love him? Did she think she was a good mother or did he? Perhaps she was just very tired like me …

Chris came back into the room carrying the glass and my

tablets. As he opened the door the light from the hall clearly illuminated his features. I felt as though I was in the darkened wing, and he was the principal actor centre stage. He certainly had the looks to be an actor – he was small but sturdy and clean-cut with that steady gaze. My eyelids were heavy but as I looked up at him I caught sight of what I thought was…

'What's that mark on the side of your face, Chris? Have you been fighting or has someone hit you?'

But I was sleepy and maybe my question was spoken too softly for him to hear. At any rate, he didn't answer but set the glass and tablets down on a small table beside me. And just before I closed my eyes again, I saw that clear gaze of Jacko and Chris fixed on me like two photographic prints that had superimposed.

SUE WILSEA

a personal essay

'What do you write *about*?' people ask politely when you tell them what you do.

My answer is always vague, 'Anything really.'

But that's not true. There are any number of subjects I'd never dare tackle – Africa, working down a mine, being an opera singer – not just because my lack of knowledge would make creating a believable reality extremely difficult but because any writing I did produce would be an empty shell.

For me, the heart of any of my stories has to be true in the sense that it must consist of something I myself have observed, experienced or felt. The process of writing consists of building around this kernel of truth and moulding it into the shape that you want. If successful, the end-product is a fiction that the reader can recognise, often albeit without realising it as 'real'. A short story cannot just be the retelling of what actually happened; if that were the case, then those people who had led interesting and exciting lives would automatically make good writers and vice versa! It involves selecting, embellishing, condensing, timing and, most importantly, deciding at what point it will start and end. Most people will

129

quite naturally go part of the way towards putting this into practice when they are telling a story to a group of friends – a little bit of exaggeration here, playing down there, omitting anything that detracts from the main point of interest and ending with the punch line. Yet how the best short stories go beyond mere anecdote is the way in which they derive some wider significance or meaning from their events. They propel the reader forward into another realm of thinking and questioning. Roald Dahl's horror stories are so good because they don't just scare, they pose questions about the dark side of human nature.

Because of the limitation of length in a short story, it often has to act as a kind of fine sieve, filtering out all but what is the essence of human experience. For example, it is very difficult to deal in elaborate characterisation or to introduce a lot of minor characters into the plot; there are similar problems involved in trying to cover large periods of time or move from place to place. A novel is better able to sprawl and stretch its limbs than a short story which tends to view life from one fixed position. However, the golden rule about short stories is that there *are* no rules, each one is unique, and if people like me try to suggest otherwise, sooner or later you will find one that successfully proves us wrong!

My short stories are like a varied collection of friends – some I have a great affection for in spite of being very aware of their weaknesses, others are more successful and we have grown apart; some are suited to a quiet mood, others enjoy company. As with friends they each highlight a different aspect of oneself. So it is with 'Double Vision': I was a teacher and came across deprived children like Jacko. As a mother too, I sometimes found it difficult to separate home and school. That's the kernel of truth; the rest is a fiction set against a background with which I'm familiar. At the same time the story allowed me to touch on themes in which I am interested – domestic violence, neglect, society's class system which is mirrored in schools, (Who do you think will be successful later on in life – a member of the Drama Group or Jacko?) You might think that I should know whether the narrator hit Chris or not (she's obviously been ill, is under a lot of pressure and her ex-husband suggests she is neurotic) or whether she has simply projected her guilt about hitting Jacko onto her son. I'm afraid I don't. Sometimes questions like that just arise in stories and don't always come supplied with answers.

The title is meant to suggest not just the woman's confusion but how everyone's view of events is different. We all look at the world and record and define it through our own mental camera – short stories are like printing some still photographs of these perceptions whereas a novel is a full-length feature film. It is always interesting to look at other people's efforts and to criticise – perhaps you would have approached the shot from a different angle, zoomed in closer or not thought it worth taking at all. However, what is far more interesting is to have a go yourself. You'll need a pen or pencil, paper and a willingness to dig out those kernels of truth. If everyone has a novel inside them just waiting to be written, as has often been said, then think how many short stories there must be!

*F*ollow On

*T*he Harry Hastings Method

BEFORE READING

CAN WE ever feel sympathy for a criminal? In what situations?

READ THE first three paragraphs. What does the writer mean by 'working the houses in the Hollywood hills'? What do you think the story will be about?

DURING READING

PAUSE AT 'Do not under any circumstances open this door!' (p 17). What do you think is there?

PAUSE AT 'a quivering mass of indecisive jelly' (p 22). What do you think is there? How do you think the story will end?

AFTER READING

MAKE A list of the ways in which the burglar broke in to Harry Hastings' house and what he took on each occasion.

WRITE THE notices you could leave in your home to put someone off entering your bedroom OR the notices you could leave to deter someone from breaking in to your school to steal the video-recorder.

WRITE A shooting script for the last section of the story, from where the burglar reads the first note about the puma on Harry Hastings' door.

DO YOU think the ending is satisfactory? Would it be more effective to finish it earlier? If so, where would be a good place to end? Try writing a different ending from the point at which the burglar is standing outside his own door wondering if there really is a puma inside.

DISCUSS THE ways in which the writer manages to make us like the burglar.

YOU ARE Harry Hastings. Write the story from your point of view.

WRITE THE story of an incompetent burglar, i.e. a burglar who isn't very good at being a burglar.

SEVERAL YEARS later you (the burglar) have become successful and well known. You are interviewed on a local radio chat show. The interviewer asks you to recall how you started out in business and how you met Harry Hastings. Work in pairs, taking it in turn to be the interviewer and the ex-burglar. This could later be recorded on audio or video-tape.

*L*ate Home

BEFORE READING

WHAT KIND of a reception do you expect if you are late home? How much difference does the time of day make, or who you've been with, or where you've been?

WHAT DEDUCTIONS can you make about the characters in the story just from the first line?

DURING READING

WHAT KIND of people do the husband and wife seem to be? Make a note of the clues you get about both their characters as you read through.

READ UP to 'The car leapt forward, roaring.' How do you think the story will end?

Pause after 'Yet I remember the sound of screaming.' Is your ending still possible? If not, how might it end?

AFTER READING

WHAT THOUGHTS go through the husband's mind as he realises what he holds in his hand?

What does he decide to say when he gets home? Write the conversation that actually takes place.

WRITE THE conversation between the husband and wife as it might have developed if he had not so quickly and completely disbelieved her. Begin where he says 'Where have you been? Do you know what time it is?' This could be done in pairs as an improvisation—or written down, the paper being swapped between partners.

AT SOME points in the story the details are very precise. (The same is true to an even greater extent in stories such as 'The Ruum' and 'The Harry Hastings Method'). The description on p 27 in the paragraph beginning 'He needs to get to the hospital' is very specific. Why did the writer think this was necessary?

THE WIFE is traced by the police and is prosecuted for causing Grievous Bodily Harm. The finger is a key exhibit.

Write the speech of the prosecuting counsel who will try to make her actions sound as bad as possible.

Write the speech of her defence counsel.

'OH, THAT'S nothing. Wait till I tell you the one about the toe!' What story might then be told? Write it or be prepared to tell it aloud.

WRITE A story called 'Late Home' which is NOT about a teenage son or daughter coming in late at night and facing the anger of parents. Perhaps you could reverse the situation and have the parents coming home late?

WHO *WERE* the figures by the side of the road? Explain what they were doing there and what happened after the woman drove off.

'*P*igs Is Pigs'

BEFORE READING

READ THE first paragraph. How do you imagine the scene? Picture the two men with the counter between them. One is called 'Mr' and one is called 'Mike'—how does this affect your impression of them?

'RULES IS rules' (page 33) is as important to this story as 'Pigs is pigs'. What are your views on rules? 'Rules are there to be broken'—is this anything more than a silly reaction to a rule someone doesn't like?

DURING READING

AT WHAT point in the story did you realise what was going to happen?

WHAT IS added to your picture of Mr Morehouse by reading up to the part where he demands the ink and his wife jumps guiltily?

AFTER READING

THIS STORY, like 'Computers Don't Argue', involves a person who has a frustrating encounter with bureaucracy. Here however, we do not have much sympathy for the person concerned. Why is this?

EXPRESS OFFICE OVERRUN
Guinea Pig Explosion
In Westcote

WRITE THREE other different headlines and sub-headlines which could begin a news report on the incidents described towards the end of the story.

WRITE A news report including all the important details to accompany one of the headlines above.

WHAT HAPPENS when the cargo of guinea pigs reaches Franklin? Write the next few pages.

Mebbe thim clerks wants me to call in the pig docther an' have their pulses took. Wan thing I do know, howiver, which is they've glorious appytites for pigs of their soize.

TRY READING the extract aloud in an appropriate accent. This is an attempt by the writer to show the speech of Mike Flannery by altering the normal spelling of some of the words. It is quite hard to do but you could try it. Think of someone you know who speaks with a distinctive accent and write a short speech in the way that he or she would say it. You may need to have several tries at this.

Here are some other examples. See if you can work out what is being said and how it is being said.

Demmertol Mogret, chep zirnia winker monda. Snort ziffy was an F I Smoshel. Feller rotterby cot moshelled. Gairdwee do things bettrin the yommy. Arrer member beckon 47, or meffpin 48. Any wet was in Tripoli. No, meffpin nelleck-zendri-yaw...

From *Fraffly Suite* by Afferbeck Lauder, Ure Smith, Sydney

'Hiyamac.'	*'Lobuddy.'*
'Binearlong?'	*'Cuplours.'*
'Ketchanenny?'	*'Goddafew.'*
'Kindarthey?'	*'Bassencarp.'*
'Enysizetoum?'	*'Cuplapouns.'*
'Hittinard?'	*'Sordalite.'*
'Wachoozin?'	*'Gobbawurms.'*
'Fishanonaboddum?'	*'Rydonnaboddum.'*
'Igoddago.'	*'Tubad.'*
'Seeyaround.'	*'Yeatakideezy.'*
'Guluk.'	

From *Ways of Talking*, ed. David Jackson, Ward Lock Educational.

In case you didn't realise, the speaker on the right is fishing and the speaker on the left is someone passing by.

LIST THE letters and notes which were written during the dispute about the rate to be charged for transporting guinea pigs. Begin:
Mr Morehouse to the President of the Interurban Express Co.
Interurban Express Co. to Mr Morehouse
Etc.

THE STORY would have been different if telephones had been in use. Act out the various communications listed above using a phone conversation in each case.

WRITE A story or a play which involves exaggeration or something which is absurd. In order for this to be successful it is advisable to have one thing in the story which is far-fetched (like the number of guinea pigs) and to keep everything else very normal.

Follow On

Crossing Over

BEFORE READING

HAVE YOU ever started out full of good intentions and gradually found that your enthusiasm disappeared? What do you do if that happens—perhaps look for an excuse to give up…or what?

DURING READING

PAUSE AT the words '…it made a hollow, echoing sound.' How do you think the story will end?

AFTER READING

THE TITLE has a double meaning; what are the two meanings?

WHEN DID you realise that the girl was a ghost? Looking back through the story, what other clues can you find which hint that she is a ghost?

WHAT HAPPENS next?

WHAT WOULD the police discover when they reached the accident? Take statements from the two drivers and any other witnesses. This can be done as a simple role play: one policeman, two drivers and a witness on the pavement:

Driver 1: you drove the yellow van which hit the girl. You are shocked, anxious not to be blamed but nevertheless feeling guilty.

Driver 2: you drove the red car which ran into the back of the van. You are angry (with the van driver, or the girl or the dog—you can decide).

Witness: you were on the pavement and saw everything. You are rather self-important and have a definite opinion on everything.

IT IS hard to write a ghost story and make it sound convincing. Write a ghost story yourself in which you keep the fact that there is a ghost in the story or that *you* are the ghost a secret from the reader for as long as possible.

WRITE TOGO'S story. You might begin like this:

> I'm a dog. They call me Togo.
> Coz I'm always ready to go.
> I'm half Alsatian
> Half something else…

137

Computers Don't Argue

BEFORE READING

THE STORY is told in an unusual way—through letters sent to and from the main character, Walter Child, as well as between other characters and agencies about him. (Some of the earliest novels—in the eighteenth century—were also written in this way!) Many of the letters Walt receives are what he calls 'form letters'. What kind of letters are these?

Some 'form letters' might be what you would call 'junk mail'. Why has that term been invented? What does most junk mail consist of? Is junk mail simply anything in which you are not interested?

FIND OUT what is meant by the word 'bureaucracy'.

DURING READING

MAKE A list of the mistakes and coincidences which lead to Walter's imprisonment.

WHAT DO you notice about the language used in form letters compared with the language used by people such as Walter Child and his lawyer?

AFTER READING

IS THIS just a light-hearted story, or is there a serious point to it?

WRITE THE next four or five letters, following the card sent by the Inter-departmental Routing Service to Governor Willikens. You will have to decide who sends what to whom.

This could be done as a group activity. Decide as a group what letters will be sent and then write one of them each.

WRITE A story entirely in the form of letters.

A BUREAUCRACY (look it up if you haven't done so already) can be like a machine. In the story, Walt feels as if he is dealing with a machine or at least something which is not really human and which will not respond to him in a normal human way. This story is a version of the science fiction tale where men and women find themselves in conflict with robots or other machines. How would Walt's experience have been different if there had been no computers or other machines involved?

INNOCENT MAN IN EXECUTION DRAMA

WRITE A newspaper story, using the above headline or one of your own invention based on 'Computers Don't Argue'. Include in it the reactions of Mike Reynolds (Walt's Attorney), Judge McDivot and Governor Willikens. Some of those involved may try to shift the blame onto other people. You may also wish to interview Samuel Grimes of the Treasure Book Club.

Alternatively, this could be an investigation carried out in groups. One person should be a radio or TV interviewer and others in the group take on the roles of McDivot, Grimes, Pruitt and so on. The interviewer should press the people being interviewed to admit some responsibility for the tragedy of Walter Child's death.

YOU ARE Walter Child. You realise that the pardon is not going to arrive on time. What happens? Write this as a story or as a script.

WHAT IF computers *did* argue? Use this as a starting point for a story or a script.

WRITE THE story of someone trying to get something put right and receiving only form letters in reply OR recount an incident from your own experience where you have a similar problem.

THERE IS a saying that 'Fire and Water are Good Servants but Bad Masters.' What does this mean?

Could computers be said to be good servants but bad masters? Write an essay on the Benefits and Disadvantages to Mankind of Machines (OR of Computers). You will need to start with a list of points to work from. For example:

BENEFITS	DISADVANTAGES
Modern machines in factories mean that people are freed from boring repetitive work.	Machines in factories have meant that more and more people are out of work.....
Cars enable us to keep in touch with friends and relations, to visit places we wouldn't otherwise see... (and so on)	Cars have caused the deaths of a huge number of people; they add to pollution; destroy the character of towns and villages... (and so on)

*H*ey *You Down There!*

BEFORE READING

IN WHAT situations can you imagine 'Hey, you down there!' being spoken or shouted?

WHAT WOULD it be like to live underground? In what ways would your life have to change?

IF PEOPLE lived without light, what would they look like? How would the way they behave be different?

HAVING READ the first four paragraphs, what impression have you got of Calvin's character? What is Dora's attitude to him?

DURING READING

THROUGHOUT THE story there are moments when Dora is reminded of something by Calvin's appearance but she cannot quite think what it is. Jot these down as they occur and see if they remind you of anything.

AFTER READING

PART OF the enjoyment of the story comes from seeing an unpleasant character come to a sticky end. What other stories can you think of where this happens?

WHAT DO we know about Glar and the people who live underground? Make a list, starting with things we can be sure about: for example, they cannot stand light.
When you run out of definite items, continue the list with things which are quite likely to be true of them but which are not specifically mentioned in the story.

YOU ARE Glar or one of the other underground dwellers. Write the story from your point of view.

WHAT EXPLANATION does Dora give to friends, neighbours, police? How will she explain Cal's disappearance (and her new wealth)? What will she do next? You could write this as a series of conversations.

FOLLOWING THE incidents in the story, there is an important meeting of the Great Council, chaired by Glar, the Master. There is a heated debate about the discovery of the world above. One side is keen to secure further supplies of chicken and turkey while the other side wishes to have no more to do with the world of light. Write this discussion as a script, inventing whatever characters you need. This could be improvised and then written up, or performed from a script you have written.

IN PAIRS: you have been appointed by Glar to plan a raid on the outer world. Work out the problems you will face and how to overcome them.

HOW DID Dora and Calvin ever come to get married? Was Calvin always as unpleasant as he now seems? If not, what made him change? If he was, why did Dora marry him? Write a biography of either Dora or Calvin which will answer these questions.

WRITE A news story about what has happened for the underground telepathic news service *Mind Of Information*.

*O*ut On The Wire

BEFORE READING

RESEARCH THE following topics: Fascism in the 1930s, Mussolini (Il Duce), Oswald Mosley and the history of Pacifism.

WHAT DOES the character 'Punch' from Punch and Judy look like? How does he behave?

TO MAKE the basic story clear, it might be useful to read it through first without any of the flashbacks, starting at the letter from the nursing home. Then it could be read again in full so that the parallels become clearer.

DURING READING

WHEN YOU read 'An old score had been well settled' what do you think has happened? Who has attacked Punch?

THE STORY contains a number of violent incidents. Make a list of them as you read through, beginning with the rugby match. At the end of the story, number the incidents in chronological order, i.e. beginning with the earliest incident in Punch's life.

AFTER READING

DISCUSS THESE questions in pairs:
- What is it that makes Punch so angry? Why?
- Do you think it's possible that Punch did insult Janet Byron?
- Does it make sense that Atkinson saved Punch?

BECAUSE OF the flashback technique and the swift cutting from one scene to the next, this story is like a film. Write a film script for all or part of 'Out On The Wire'.

THE PHYSICAL pain of the barbed wire is matched by Punch's mental anguish at the end of the story. Describe what is going through his mind at that point.

WRITE A story using the technique of flashback.

WRITE A biography of Edward Roundtree based on the information in the story. You may invent one or two things to give his life-story more substance if you wish.

APART FROM some aspects of their appearance, are there any similarities between Edward Roundtree and the traditional character of 'Punch'?

LIKE 'Double Vision' this story moves backwards and forwards in time. Which of the flashbacks have parallels in Punch's later life?

Are there times in your life which you tend to remember vividly? Particular incidents from your past could be told to a partner, a group or the class. Little stories of this sort are called *anecdotes* and are often funny—or are told in an amusing way, however serious the original event itself may have been. Each person in a small group can relate an anecdote to the rest of the group and then write down someone else's story.

An Incident In The Ghobashi Household

BEFORE READING

READ THE first three paragraphs. Where do you think the story is set?

WHAT, APART from the writer's name, might make you think that the writer came from the country where the story takes place— rather than just having visited it or read about it?

DURING READING

AS YOU read through, make a list of unfamiliar words. When you have finished, write down what you think each one probably means.

STOP AT the point where Zeinat says 'Let's find some solution before your father returns.' How do you think the story will carry on?

AFTER READING

THE WRITER never says 'Ni'ma is pregnant'. Note down the phrases and sentences the writer uses in order to indicate:
— Zeinat's awareness that Ni'ma is pregnant
— Zeinat's question to Ni'ma about how long she has been pregnant
— Zeinat's question to Ni'ma about trying to abort the pregnancy.

HOW DOES Zeinat react to the fact that her daughter is pregnant: astonished, calm, delighted, hopeless, thoughtful, inventive, angry, generous, panicky...? Choose the best words to describe how she reacts and add some of your own if you can.

How does Ni'ma feel? Look especially at the conversation on the third page.

DISCUSS THESE questions in pairs:
— What is the importance of the old clothes mentioned towards the end of the story?
— Think about the actions and conversation of the two women. What does it suggest about the character and attitudes of Ni'ma's father, Ghobashi?
— What other clues about his attitudes and beliefs are there?

IN SPITE of the foreign setting, the basic experiences of the mother and daughter are much the same as those in our own culture. What is similar and what is different? If you set the story in Britain, what (apart from little details) would you have to change?

GHOBASHI COMES home earlier than expected. It also happens to be the night that Ni'ma is expected back with her baby. Write what happens in the form of a story or a script.

WRITE A story in which one parent assists a child with a problem, knowing that the other parent would be angry or upset.

*T*he Ruum

BEFORE READING

PAUSE AFTER the first sentence. What deduction can you make about what sort of a story this will be?
Pause after '...it was the age of reptiles.' What can you deduce about what a ruum might be?
Pause after '...no gloomy forebodings.' What on earth is going to happen?

DURING READING

NOTICE THE use of precise detail, e.g. 'maximum radius 30 miles and 160 pounds plus or minus 15' and 'each specimen was about the size of a large sheep.' Collect some other examples of detail.

MAKE A list of the skills Jim Irwin makes use of during the story. What knowledge and training does he have which come in useful?

AFTER READING

WITH A partner discuss why the ruum did not add Jim to its collection.

FIND OUT the meanings of 'implacable' and 'dispassionate'. What other words would describe the ruum well?

BASING YOUR work on descriptions in the story, draw and label a ruum. List the abilities it has.

DRAW A sketch map of Jim's route from the place where he saw the collection of beasts to where the ruum caught up with him. There are details in the story you can make use of but you will need to use your imagination as well.

HOW MANY different ways did Jim try to stop the ruum? List them, describing each one briefly.

JIM'S FEELINGS change throughout the story. How many different emotions can you detect?

THE WRITER makes clever use of *time* and *detail*.
If you made a list of details earlier, look at it now and underline items which were necessary for the plot. For example, the fact that the ruum is described as 'self-energising' on the first page explains why it kept going for so long. Why is the fire-fight included (also on the first page)? What else is put in because it will be needed later on in the story?
Some details are included simply to make the story more believable, to add to its realism, e.g. 'a hollow, sting-like probe, dripping with greenish liquid, poised snakily between them.' Find four or five other examples if you haven't done so already. (Next time you write, include enough details to make *your* writing believable.)
Notice also how the writer uses *time*. This is how the first couple of pages is organised:

Conversation aboard the space ship	half page
Events some time later	one paragraph
Conversation between Jim and Walt, millions of years later	quarter page
Background telling us Jim's purpose	one paragraph
Details of his preparation	one paragraph
The passing of over two weeks and an explanation of what Jim is about to do	one paragraph

From here the rest of the story is concerned with the events of just one day! A writer can cover a year (or a few million years) in a paragraph and expand an hour to fill several pages, depending on how he or she wants to tell the story. When you write *your* next story, think about how you will allocate the time that passes in it.

Bearing in mind the points about time and detail, plan and write a story of your own which involves a chase. It might be interesting to make one of the participants non-human.

Analyse the use of time or detail in another short story.

OBVIOUSLY THE writer invented things such as the ruum and the space ship but elsewhere it's clear that he had some very useful knowledge that helped him to write the story. What examples of this can you find?

IF THE ruum could talk, what would it say?

THIS WOULD be a big story when the media eventually found out about it.

Write four different headlines for four different newspapers.

Write the first sentence for the newscaster on the main TV news bulletin and for a local radio station.

Write the news story as it appears under one of your headlines or as it runs on after one of your introductory sentences.

Interview Jim Irwin about his amazing experiences. This could be recorded straight away or after some rehearsal.

SCIENTISTS, ESPECIALLY military scientists, will want to examine the ruum. Write the story of their mission to capture it.

T*he Cure*

BEFORE READING

WHAT SUPERSTITIONS exist in your community? Ones like not walking under a ladder are common, but do you know of any which are unusual, perhaps restricted to your family or to your part of the country?

WHEN WAS hanging abolished as a penalty for stealing in Britain?

DURING READING

PAUSE AFTER 'I don't want to go,' he mumbled. 'I don't want to.' What do you think the story is going to be about?

Pause again after 'and keep your eyes shut at the end.' Does this alter your idea of what the story will be about?

AFTER READING

IN PAIRS, discuss the following questions:
— What is it that the boy needs to be cured of?
— What does local superstition recommend as a cure?
— Does it work in Davie's case?
— How do you know?
— Why does his mother agree to take him for 'the cure'?
— Why was Davie's father hanged?

WHAT WORDS are used to describe the villagers, Davie and the mother? Make three lists, beginning like this:

Villagers	Davie	Mother
'calling and crowding'	'little more than a	'anger at the
'itching to get away	baby'	neighbours'
up the hill'	'snivelling'	
		...and so on

WRITE SHORT descriptions of the villagers, Davie and his mother based on the information you have listed plus any other deductions you can make from the story. The villagers are very important in the tale and should be given careful attention, their good points and their bad.

THE WRITER does not reveal what is happening until a page or two into the story. At what point did you realise
— that something strange was going to happen?
— that Davie was going to be touched by his hanged father?
— that the story was set in a past century?

WITHOUT MODERN news media the story of Dick Weir and his son Davie would be passed from village to village by word of mouth, perhaps by travelling merchants.

Tell the story of Dick and Davie to a crowd of interested listeners in a nearby village. Make up any details you don't know.

Now write the story as it might appear in a modern newspaper.

S*ee Me In Me Benz And T'ing*

BEFORE READING

FIND OUT about the recent history of Jamaica and the sort of problems it faces.

WHAT FEELINGS are aroused by the first sentence of the story?

DURING READING

IN THE first half page the following words are used in connection with the Lady: angrily, complained, annoyance, ordered, pouted. What do these suggest about her character? Make a note of similar words later in the story.

'LIKE WILD animals some of them, with their uncombed heads and crazy talk' is how the Lady thinks of the people in the city. Make a list of the other unpleasant images the Lady uses about people in the rest of the story.

AFTER READING

WHAT WORDS sum up the Lady? Spoilt, selfish...? How many can you think of which are really accurate descriptions of her character?

IN PAIRS, discuss the following questions:
— Why does the crowd destroy her car?
— Why does the story have the subtitle 'Like the Lady Who Lived On That Isle Remote'?
— What similarities are there between this story and the story of the Good Samaritan?
— Is the Lady a real character or just a caricature or a stereotype? (If you haven't come across these words before, ask your teacher to explain them.) Has the writer made her too unpleasant?
— 'As if she were personally responsible for the squalor in which they lived.' The Lady obviously feels no responsibility at all towards the poor of the city. Should she feel some responsibility?
— Think about the ending and the actions of the two old women. What point is the writer trying to make? Will the Lady appreciate what they do? Will she be changed at all by her experiences?

THINK ABOUT the sort of person Carl is, from the evidence in the story. Write the story of Carl's day, giving as much attention to his thoughts and feelings as the writer does to the Lady's.

THE LADY'S friends gather. Write their conversation. Here is a possible beginning:

'My dear! Did you hear about poor Annie?'
'I heard she'd had some kind of accident.'
'Accident! Well, you could call it that...'

You could write this as a script. Whichever way you write it, the dialogue should last for at least one minute. This and the item following could be improvised first and then written up, or performed from a script after a first or final draft.

YOU ARE a reporter first on the scene of the riot. Interview four or five different people about what happened, including at least one who was involved in the attack on the Lady's car. The people trust you and will speak quite openly to you.

YOU ARE a reporter whom the people do not trust. Write what the people tell you.

IN THIS situation the Mercedes Benz is seen as a status symbol and as a symbol of privilege. What things might a poor person in Britain see as symbols of status or privilege?

*D*ouble Vision

BEFORE READING

FIND OUT what 'double vision' is. Bear this in mind as you read the story.

WHAT IS a runt?

DURING READING

THERE ARE some difficult words in this story, mainly because the writer is trying to deal with feelings which are difficult to describe or explain. Don't worry about the words you don't understand; jot them down and they can be dealt with later.

THE STORY moves backwards and forwards in time. Be prepared for this as you are reading.

WHEN YOU have read as far as '...he had left us for good' you have learnt a good deal about the narrator and her background. What can you say about her from the evidence so far?

AFTER READING

CHILDREN, IN school or at home, can be infuriating. Describe in writing or to a partner the following:
— an occasion when you have been deliberately infuriating
— a time when you were infuriating without even realising it.
  If you are so perfect or your memory is so bad that you cannot do this, describe a time when someone has infuriated *you*.

IN PAIRS, discuss the following questions:
— Why does the narrator link the two boys, Jacko and Chris, so closely in her mind?
— Both Jacko and Chris make her feel rather guilty. Why do you think she feels guilty?
— Towards the end of the story the writer uses a flashback about Christmas presents. What feeling is she trying to evoke in the reader by relating this incident? Why does she want to create that feeling at this point in the story?
— Why was the teacher so upset that she had to leave and go home?

WRITE THE rest of the story as it might have continued if the teacher had not made an excuse and gone home.

THE TIME sequence in this story is quite complicated. It begins by going back over the past in a general way, describing the class and Jacko, and then reaches the present where the narrator says 'On this particular occasion...' But then, almost immediately, there is a flashback to earlier that morning, a further flashback to several months before, a return to the morning and then to the occasion which is the focus of the story. Write a story, perhaps based on an incident from your own life, in which you use several layers of time

Follow On

and memory in a similar way. It isn't easy and it will need careful planning before you start.

WRITE 'Jacko's Story' or 'Chris' Story'.

The only thing they understand is a clip round the ear!
Bring back the cane, that's what I say. It's the only thing some of them understand.

THESE OPINIONS are heard in many school staffrooms. What sort of teachers say things like this? Are they right? Should corporal punishment be allowed in schools? Prepare an argument for or against its use.

WRITE A conversation between several teachers who disagree on the issue of corporal punishment. This could be improvised first and then written up, or performed from the script you have written.

Earlier that morning, Chris, my son, and I had clawed at each other's feelings in the way that only people who are close to each other do.

WE OFTEN feel complicated and mixed feelings for people we are close to: both loving someone like a brother, sister, parent or child but also being moved to fury, almost hatred of them at times. Either describe a person for whom you have such feelings or write a story in which such feelings play a central part.

WHAT WOULD you have felt if your mother had said to you 'Do you think I'm a good mother?' What are the characteristics of a good mother, or of a good father? Do they necessarily have to be different characteristics? How would you answer the question, 'Are you a good son/daughter?'

WRITE AN article for a magazine with the title 'How To Be A Perfect Mother/Father/Son/Daughter'.

THERE ARE three different conflicts in the story: mother-son, wife-husband and teacher-pupil. Which of these affects the narrator most, and why?

'JACKO HAD gripped a stub of pencil in his fist...' Why does this choice of words have a different effect to 'Jacko held a short pencil in his hand'? What effect does the phrase 'dug into' have, later in the sentence? Notice that it is the *choice* of words which makes all the difference to a piece of writing.

151

Further Ideas For Group Work

The items which follow could be undertaken by pairs or groups, though there is no reason why most of them could not be adapted for individual work.

The first section may be useful as a way into some of the more difficult stories immediately after they have been read. Additional statements can of course be inserted or whole batches created—perhaps by pupils—for those stories not dealt with here.

In pairs or small groups discuss how far you agree with the statements which follow. Give a score of 1 if you agree completely, a 2 if you agree, but not wholeheartedly, a 3 if you mildly disagree and a 4 if you strongly disagree.

'PIGS IS PIGS'

1 Mr Morehouse is a kind father.
2 Mr Morehouse has a high opinion of himself.
3 Mike Flannery thought it would be a straightforward task to get Mr Morehouse to pay for the food eaten by the guinea-pigs.
4 Mike Flannery would have saved himself a lot of trouble if he had not stuck to the letter of the rules book.
5 The experience with the guinea-pigs makes Mike Flannery bitter and angry.

OUT ON THE WIRE

1 Punch's experiences in the war have made him detest all violence.
2 Punch expects boys to be cruel.
3 Because of his physical disabilities Punch is unable to win the respect of the boys.
4 Atkinson shows only ignorance and prejudice in his attitudes towards the French.
5 Punch is in love with Janet Byron.
6 Punch's beliefs are very similar to Mussolini's, so he would be keen to teach Italian.

INCIDENT IN THE GHOBASHI HOUSEHOLD

1 Zeinat is angry when she discovers Ni'ma is pregnant.
2 Zeinat is likely to be worried that she has not carried out her husband's instructions to take care of Ni'ma.
3 Ni'ma is unconcerned about her pregnancy.

4 Zeinat is a generous and thoughtful mother.
5 Zeinat is a deceitful woman who is encouraging her daughter to misbehave.
6 Ghobashi sounds like an understanding and tolerant father.

THE RUUM

1 The ruum had been left behind to collect specimens.
2 Jim Irwin needs to strike uranium because he is short of money and he has a wife who is pregnant to support.
3 If the ruum had picked him up when it first detected him, Jim would have become part of the line of paralysed creatures.
4 The ruum is a very intelligent and well-equipped creature.
5 The ruum is a highly sophisticated killing machine.
6 Jim Irwin never panicked and never despaired.
7 The chase lasted well over twelve hours.
8 It is not likely that other humans had visited the area.

SEE ME IN ME BENZ AND T'ING

1 The Lady admires expensive possessions.
2 She sympathises with those who are poorer than herself.
3 She finds the inhabitants of the poorer parts of the city physically unpleasant.
4 The Lady doesn't like to feel cut off from the life going on around her.
5 Once she had escaped from the car, the Lady wasn't too bothered about it.
6 The Lady is lucky to be rescued by the two old friends.

DOUBLE VISION

1 The class liked Jacko because he entertained them.
2 Chris and his mother do not get on well together.
3 The teacher was glad she had won the respect of Jacko by striking him.
4 The teacher hit Jacko because she was already upset and his imitation of her was the last straw.
5 The teacher has no feelings towards Jacko except intense dislike.
6 The only similarity between Jacko and Chris is their height.

Taking the collection as a whole, make decisions on the following items as a group.

1 Which of the stories have something serious to say—a message or a moral—and which are just for fun/entertainment/the pleasure of telling a good tale? Divide them into two lists.

2 *Survival* is a common theme. It can take many forms, perhaps even that of battling with the demands of countless guinea-pigs. Make a list of the stories in which the theme of survival occurs and say what form it takes in each. For example:

'The Ruum'   Escaping from the clutches of the robot 'ruum'

3 In 'The Harry Hastings Method' the burglar says 'Susie told us in class that in every story there is like a moment of decision.' The moments of decision for him are fairly obvious! How many other moments of decision can you find in the rest of the stories?

4 In most stories the writer seems to have a strong sympathy with the main character. This is not so in all of them and this can give a story an extra 'edge'. In which stories does the writer seem *not* to be in sympathy with the main character he or she has created?

Decide *separately* which story would make the best stage play, the best film, the best radio play and the best comic strip. Which would be the hardest to turn into any other form apart from a story? When you have done this, compare your list with others in your group and see if you agree upon a final list. Be prepared to explain your choices.

The illustration which accompanied the original publication of 'Late Home' consisted of a close-up of an index finger just in front of a clock-face. Draw title page illustrations for two of the other stories in the collection. Make sure each person in the group is working on a different story.

Prepare a dramatised reading—complete with sound effects and music—of one of the stories. As each group will need to practise their reading separately, this can only be done effectively if there is adequate space available.

EXTENDED STUDY ON BEGINNINGS AND ENDINGS

Beginnings and endings are key elements in short stories. Several of the stories begin with the names of characters: 'Susie Plimson says...', 'Mike Flannery, the Westcote agent of...' or 'Calvin Spender drained his coffee cup...' This is a method of giving information to the reader and getting on with the story straight away. Other stories begin abruptly: ' "Runt, runt!" the kids would jeer...' or 'Where was she this time?...' or 'Mud stuck to his face, clogging his mouth...' This is a way of getting attention and arousing the reader's curiosity.

Endings are also extremely important in short stories, probably more important than beginnings. Most of the stories in this collection have endings which are crucial to the rest of the story. In other words, the whole story depends on the way it ends. Many of the stories could be said to have a 'twist' or 'sting in the tail', whether a sharp one (as in 'Late Home'), a mild one (as in 'Incident In The Ghobashi Household') or one you have to think about (as in 'The Ruum').

LOOK AGAIN at some other beginnings and endings and see what other methods writers have used.

SOME STORIES spring from an incident in the writer's life or an incident which he or she has heard about. Others come from wondering along the lines of 'What would happen if...?' Think again about the stories in this book and in each case make a suggestion about how the story might have originated.

MOST SHORT stories use only a few characters and extend over a fairly short stretch of time, unless they make use of the flashback technique as in 'Out On The Wire'. Which story has the fewest characters and which has the most? Which story covers the shortest period of time and which (apart from those using flashback) covers the longest?

PLAN AND then write your next story bearing in mind all the points that have just been made. It could be a good one!

EXTENDED STUDY ON RELATIONSHIPS

Relationships between people are the central theme of most fiction, and these stories are no exception. Many include a married couple and several of them do not present marriage in a favourable light. Of other relationships, the parent-child one is the most common.

WHICH OF the stories has the most positive view of married life and which has the most negative? Arrange the remainder in order of positive to negative.

WHICH STORIES deal with parenthood? In which is the parent-child relationship the best; in which is it the worst?

RELATIONSHIPS OFTEN involve conflict. It has been said that there is no drama without conflict. Is this true? Think about the stories in this collection and see what kinds of conflict are involved in them. In 'Double Vision', for example, there are conflicts between mother and son and between teacher and pupil.

ARE THERE any stories in this collection which do not have a conflict as one of the basic elements?

THINK ABOUT what would happen if characters from different stories met. Mike Flannery meets The Lady... The burglar meets Calvin Spender...
 Either plan and then write a story in which two or more characters from different stories meet.
 Or plan and then write a story (based on your own experience or that of people you know) in which relationships form the basis of the plot. Conflict between certain characters will probably play a part.

Further Reading

Any selection of follow-up reading is bound to be arbitrary. The suggestions below are personal recommendations rather than an academic bibliography. Details of publishers are given at the end of this section where titles are listed alphabetically.

'The Harry Hastings Method' is reminiscent of stories about confidence tricksters. O. Henry wrote a number of amusing tales involving such characters, including 'The Science Of Matrimony'. See also his story 'The Ransom Of Red Chief' in *Sweet and Sour*, another volume in this short story series. Also recommended are 'Little Old Lady From Cricket Creek' by Len Gray and 'Jean Labadie's Big Black Dog' by Natalie Carlson.

If you enjoyed 'Late Home' you will probably like many of the stories by Roald Dahl. The anthology *Twisters* provides several stories with a similar feel to them and it would be worth taking a look at *Dead of Night—Stories of the Macabre* edited by Peter Haining.

'Pigs Is Pigs' is a tale of mounting absurdity which is reflected in such stories as 'The Loaded Dog' by Henry Lawson and 'The Battle Of Bubble And Squeak' by Philippa Pearce. 'Rats' by J.B.S. Haldane also makes a good comparison.

'Crossing Over' contains some of the same elements as 'Late Home'. The supernatural will be found in hundreds of tales with ghostly connections—see, for instance, 'The Birthday Present' by Marjorie Darke and collections by Joan Aiken, e.g. *A Touch of Chill*, and Vivien Alcock, e.g. *Ghostly Companions*.

'Computers Don't Argue' has a certain amount in common with other computer/robot/machine stories, which are usually science fiction. 'A Lot To Learn' by Robert Kurosawa (*Twisters*) is amusing. 'Examination Day' by Henry Sleasar (*Twisters*) and 'Who Can Replace A Man?' by Brian W. Aldiss are more serious and thought-provoking. Isaac Asimov is one of the best known authors of science fiction novels in which robots feature as main characters.

The best follow-up to 'Out On The Wire' is First World War poetry rather than prose fiction (see especially the work of Wilfred Owen, Siegfried Sassoon and Isaac Rosenberg) though *All Quiet on the Western Front* by Erich Remarque is still well worth reading, as are extracts from Robert Graves' *Goodbye to All That*.

Many Roald Dahl stories echo the macabre humour of 'Hey You Down There!' The underground element is captured in two books written many years ago: *The Machine Stops* by E.M. Forster and the section in H.G. Wells' *Time Machine* which deals with the Morlocks.

To follow up the issue of unwanted pregnancy in 'Incident In The

Ghobashi Household', read *Young Mother* by Josephine Kamm, *It's My Life* by Robert Leeson, *Getting Free* by Nigel Hinton and *A Kind of Loving* by Stan Barstow. The aspect of cultural differences is further pursued in Rukshana Smith's *Sumitra's Story* or Buchi Emecheta's *Second-Class Citizen*.

'The Ruum' combines a chase/escape story with science fiction. If you enjoy science fiction, then you will probably like the work of John Christopher (author of the *Tripods* trilogy and many others), Monica Hughes (*Ring Rise, Ring Set, The Keeper of the Isis Light* and many others) and Nicholas Fisk. The variety of writing within science fiction is very great so if one writer doesn't suit you, try another. For stories with a chase or escape element, try 'The Most Dangerous Game' by Richard Connell or 'Trapped' by Liam O'Flaherty. Robot stories can be found in many science fiction collections, some of which are noted above, in relation to 'Computers Don't Argue'.

The theme of witches and superstition dealt with in 'The Cure' is perhaps less common. *Witch Child* and *A Walk to See the King* by Rony Robinson are both well written. There are many non-fiction books on the subject but they vary in quality. *A Circle of Witches* by Peter Haining is worth looking at and you might find the descriptive essay 'A Hanging' by George Orwell interesting.

The issues raised by 'See Me In Me Benz And T'ing' have more to do with class than racial conflict. *Heritage*, a Caribbean anthology, *Over Our Way* and *Carribbean Stories* could enlarge your understanding of the West Indian world. See also 'The Best Day of My Easter Holidays' by Jane Gardam and the writing of Langston Hughes.

There are many stories which deal with the problems between parents and children! *The Summer of My German Soldier* by Bette Greene is worth reading; *Edith Jackson* by Rosa Guy and *Nobody's Family Is Going To Change* by Louise FitzHugh give fresh insights. The collections *Wayward Girls and Wicked Women*, *Breaking Away* and the Spare Rib Reader would be useful books to dip into for other perspectives on issues raised by the situation of the woman in *Double Vision*.

A Circle Of Witches, Peter Haining, Robert Hale
'A Hanging' by George Orwell in *Essays*, Penguin
A Kind Of Loving, Stan Barstow, Heinemann
All Quiet On The Western Front, Erich Remarque, Heinemann
A Roald Dahl Selection, ed. Roy Blatchford, Longman
A Touch Of Chill, Joan Aiken, Fontana
A Walk To See The King, Rony Robinson, Nelson
Breaking Away, ed. Davies and Morland, Longman
Caribbean Stories, ed. Morland, Longman
Dead of Night, Peter Haining, Kimber
Edith Jackson, Rosa Guy, Puffin

Getting Free, Nigel Hinton, Heinemann

Ghostly Companions, Vivien Alcock, Fontana

Goodbye To All That, Robert Graves, Penguin

Heritage, ed. Esmor Jones, Cassell

I'm The King Of The Castle, Susan Hill, Longman

It's My Life, Robert Leeson, Fontana

'Jean Labadie's Big Black Dog' by Natalie Carlson in *The Blue Storyhouse*, ed. Jackson and Pepper, Oxford

'Little Old Lady From Cricket Creek' by Len Gray in *Twisters* and *The Quickening Pulse*, ed. D. J. Brindley, Hodder & Stoughton

Nobody's Family Is Going To Change, Louise FitzHugh, MacMillan

Over Our Way, ed. D'Costa and Pollard, Longman

Portraits, Kate Chopin, The Women's Press

'Rats' by J. B. S. Haldane in *The Quickening Pulse*, ed. D. J. Brindley, Hodder & Stoughton

Second-Class Citizen, Buchi Emecheta, Fontana

Shane, Jack Schaefer, Heinemann

Stepping Out, ed. Jane Leggett, Unwin Hyman

Sumitra's Story, Rukshana Smith, Bodley Head

That Crazy April, Katherine Paterson, Puffin

The Battle Of Bubble And Squeak, Philippa Pearce, Puffin

'The Best Day Of My Easter Holidays' by Jane Gardam in *Other Places, Other Worlds*, ed. R. Jones, Heinemann

'The Birthday Present' by Marjorie Darke in *Sweet and Sour*, Unwin Hyman

The Great Gilly Hopkins, Katherine Paterson, Puffin

The Hobbit, J. R. R. Tolkien, Unwin Hyman

'The Loaded Dog' by Henry Lawson in *Other Places, Other Worlds*, ed. R. Jones, Heinemann

'The Machine Stops' by E. M. Forster in *Twentieth Century Short Stories*, ed. Barnes and Egford, Harrap

'The Most Dangerous Game' by Richard Connell in *American Short Stories*, Longman

The Never-ending Story, Michael Ende, Puffin

'The Science Of Matrimony' by O. Henry in *Storytellers 2*, ed. R. Mansfield, Schofield & Sims

The Summer Of My German Soldier, Bette Greene, Puffin

The Time Machine, H. G. Wells, Pan

'Trapped' by Liam O'Flaherty in *Story 2*, ed. Jackson and Pepper, Penguin

Twisters, ed. Steve Bowles, Fontana

Witch Child, Rony Robinson, Nelson

'Who Can Replace A Man?' by Brian W. Aldiss in *The World Around Us*, ed. R. Jones, Heinemann

Wayward Girls And Wicked Women, ed. Angela Carter, Virago

Young Mother, Josephine Kamm, Heinemann

Acknowledgements

The editor and publisher would like to express thanks for permission to reprint the following stories in this anthology:

'The Harry Hastings' Method' © Warner Law 1971, reprinted by permission of Carol Russell Law.

'Late Home' and personal essay © Trevor Millum.
'Late Home' was first published in *Traffic Island and Other Stories* (G. Brash, S'pore 1984)

'Crossing Over' © Catherine Storr, reprinted by permission of Faber and Faber Limited.

'Computers Don't Argue' © Gordon Dickson, Arnold Thomson Publishers, California.

'Hey You Down There!' © Harold Rolseth, published by Fontana Lions, an imprint of Collins Publishers, London.

'Out On The Wire' and personal essay © David Harmer.

'An Incident In The Ghobashi Household' © Alifa Rifaat from *Distant View of A Minaret*, published by Quartet Books Ltd.

'The Ruum' © Arthur Porges, Mercury House Publishing, San Francisco.

'See Me In Me Benz And T'ing © Hazel Campbell.

Double Vision and personal essay © Sue Wilsea.
'Double Vision' was first published in *Proof*, the LHA Literary Magazine.

Although every effort has been made to contact the copyright-holders this has not proved to be possible in every case. We apologise for any unwitting infringements of copyright.